Monkey Business

Also by Anna Wilson

Puppy Love
Pup Idol
Puppy Power

Kitten Kaboodle
Kitten Smitten
Kitten Cupid

And chosen by Anna Wilson
Fairy Stories
Princess Stories

Monkey Business

Anna Wilson

ILLUSTRATED BY MOIRA MUNRO

MACMILLAN CHILDREN'S BOOKS

First published 2011 by Macmillan Children's Books
a division of Macmillan Publishers Limited
20 New Wharf Road, London N1 9RR
Basingstoke and Oxford
Associated companies throughout the world
www.panmacmillan.com

ISBN 978-0-330-50928-2

1 3 5 7 9 8 6 4 2

A CIP catalogue record for this book is available from
the British Library.

Printed and bound in the UK by CPI Mackays, Chatham ME5 8TD

For Thomas and William,
who never did get their own zoo . . .

CONTENTS

CONTENTS

1
IN THE
ANIMAL HOUSE

'Felix, ARE you listening to me? Hel-lo-oh?'

Mum had pinched her nose between forefinger and thumb and was speaking in what was supposed to be an astronauty sort of voice.

'Mother ship calling Planet Felix! Is there any life on Planet Felix?'

Felix blinked slowly and looked at Mum. Why did she think talking like that was funny? It actually only made her look embarrassingly weird. He carried on crunching his Monster Pops breakfast cereal slowly and with Great Concentration. It took Great Concentration to keep his mouth that full as the cereal kept trying to pop out. Also it was extremely important that he keep his mouth totally full like that so that he didn't have to answer

1

Awkward Questions, such as the ones Mum was asking now.

'FELIX!'

Mum was actually yelling.

Felix also noticed that her cheeks had gone kind of beetrooty red.

It dawned on him that Mum was probably not trying to be funny after all.

'Ooh!' Mum growled in frustration. 'LISTEN TO ME! I asked you why you thought your school coat was a great place to keep a snail. A LIVE snail! Isn't it enough that you filled the bath with frogspawn last week? I am taking this slimy mollusc back to where it belongs—'

It was at that moment that Felix noticed the thing Mum was holding in the hand that hadn't been pinching her nose. It had the effect of flicking a switch in his brain, and he leaped from the table, shouting through a mouthful of cereal, 'Give him back!'

He lunged and grabbed the Superb Specimen that Mum was dangling in front of his face. 'That's Bernard. I found him yesterday on the pavement. Someone would have stepped on him if I hadn't saved him!' he protested.

'How do you know it's a he?' sniggered Merv, Felix's older brother.

'*Don't*,' Mum said to Merv with feeling.

But Felix wasn't listening. He was stroking Bernard's shell. He had meant to put him in a pot in his bedroom and give him some of those spiky leaves to eat: the ones growing out of the pavement near where he'd found Bernard. But somehow something had got Felix distracted, so Bernard had spent the night in his coat pocket instead.

Mum should at least be pleased that he had changed his mind about putting Bernard in his *pyjama* pocket, Felix thought. If the state of that rather, well, *flattened* ladybird was anything to go by earlier this morning, Bernard might have come to a very sticky end indeed . . .

Felix sighed.

Mum was still squawking about there being a 'Place for Everything and Everything in its Place'.

Felix curled his top lip. *Everyone* knew that the place for a snail was in the garden, but everyone *also* knew (in this family anyway) that Mum Did Not Like Snails in the Garden. Knowing this, surely it was reasonable to assume that Mum should prefer having snails *indoors*? In fact, the more he thought of it, the more Felix persuaded himself that he had done Mum a favour by adopting Bernard.

Felix wondered for a tiny micro-nanosecond if he should say as much, but the minute that thought came to an end, Mum's eyebrows locked into One-Eyebrow Mode and her eyes shone like the eyes of that rather scary silver-backed gorilla on the poster in his room.

4

'Aha!' he said under his breath. 'That reminds me. I need that book on apes to show at school.' And, shoving Bernard into the pocket of his shorts, he pushed back his chair mumbling, 'Sorry, Mum – just forgot something.' He was concentrating so hard on avoiding looking into her scary eyes that he accidentally trod on the dog.

'YOWP!' yelped Dyson. He had been under the table as usual, snoozing and waiting for crumbs.

'Sorry, Dyson,' said Felix, patting his dog's head and elbowing the cat in the face by mistake.

'MIIIIAAAAOW!' complained Colin. He had been about to pounce on Dyson and now he'd missed his chance.

'Sorry, Colin,' said Felix, reaching over to stroke the cat, and catching the end of his spoon with his sleeve.

5

'Feeee–liiiix!' Mum yelled as his cereal bowl clattered to the floor. 'Leave those blasted animals alone for once and make your teeth and clean your bed and brush your shoes and GET YOUR HAIR ON! We're going to be LATE!'

'I'm off then,' muttered Dad, ramming on his cycle helmet and backing away from the chaos. He picked up a banana and jammed his mobile phone into his backpack. He put the banana to his ear.

'I'll be there in five,' he said into the banana.

Mum's face had reached boiling point. Her teeth were actually bared like a real live lion's.

'Sorry, Mum,' said Felix, stumbling out of the kitchen. He caught the edge of the overcrowded work surface behind him and narrowly missed knocking over the hamster cage. Hammer squeaked furiously. 'Sorry, Hammer,' said Felix. 'Are you all right?'

'Felix,' Mum said in a dangerously low tone.

'I'm going, I'm going,' he said.

'For good?' Merv sneered through his greasy fringe. 'I'll help you pack.'

'MERVIN!' Mum screeched. 'DON'T START!'

This was what you might call an average morning in the Stowe household. Felix rocketed up the stairs two at a time thinking that he really was the only sane person in the whole entire family (well, the human bit of it, anyway).

'Life would be much more fun and interesting if I was a monkey,' Felix said aloud as he scooted around his room looking for the book on apes. 'Monkeys live in family groups, but I bet no one ever tells *them* that they have to clean their teeth or go to school or eat broccoli.'

He hurled dirty pants and socks and wildlife magazines and bits of Lego over his shoulder as he searched for the book. Ah, there it was – stuffed underneath his box of precious things, in between the dried-up frog and the squashed dragonfly. He tucked the book under one arm, being careful not to squash Bernard – dragonflies were still nice to look at when they were squashed, but snails were definitely not.

'Since I can't be a monkey,' he muttered, ambling to the bathroom, 'maybe I can at least get myself adopted by a family who likes animals?' He was thinking aloud about this and about the marvellous things that animals do when he walked into the bathroom and came face to face with Merv, who was on the loo.

'Get out, squirt!' said Merv.

'Phoooar!' Felix roared, flapping his hands theatrically. 'It stinks in here!'

'GET OUT!' Merv thundered.

'Actually, your stinkiness has just reminded me of something incredibly interesting, Merv,' said

Felix, grinning wickedly.

After all, Merv couldn't get at him from his current position. He was what you might call a Captured Audience.

'Did you know that cows produce something from their bottoms called methane gas, which is a posh way of saying that they fart a lot?' Felix continued. 'Even more than you do! And did you know that cows will probably one day rule the planet, as the ozone layer is filling up with their farts? So that means we are all breathing in cow farts every day and we humans will probably die because of that? And then only cows will be left in the world. Aren't cows amazing?'

'You *are* a fart,' Merv yelled. 'GET OUT!'

Felix blew a raspberry at his brother and hurtled out to the downstairs loo. 'Doesn't *anyone* in this family think it's cool that we are actually breathing in cow farts every day?' he muttered, tripping over

Dyson, who was snoozing at the bottom of the stairs, and falling heavily on Colin, who had been lying in wait again.

'YEEEEOOOOWL!' screeched the cat.

Felix picked himself up and chucked his book on the floor. He carefully checked that Bernard was still in one unsquashed piece, and then went into the cloakroom and shut the door behind him.

'Sorry, Bernard,' he whispered.

Felix sighed heavily at his reflection in the mirror. No one understood him. Take last night for another example: all he had done was say that he would like a gecko as a pet. Merv had burped loudly and said, 'What's that? Some kind of robot?' and Mum had said, 'I am NOT, repeat NOT having any more animals in this house. A dog, a cat, a hamster and a goldfish (OK, an ex-goldfish, but, still, you know what I mean) are quite enough, not to mention the snails and spiders . . . Oh, and not forgetting the frogspawn . . .'

'But, Mum, Jonah the goldfish died *weeks* ago. And you said I had to let the frogspawn go because it was turning the bath all slimy,' Felix reminded her. 'And it's so *boring* only having normal pets.'

'BORING?' Mum snapped. '*Boring?* If only life *were* boring, that's what I say. Give me a bit of *boring* any day of the week . . .' And then she'd gone off on one about how all she ever seemed to do these days was 'feed animals, walk animals and clean up after animals and if you think . . .'

Oh, it was even too *boring* to try to remember what else Mum had said.

By now he was deeply engrossed in concocting a plan to make his life more interesting and his family more animal-minded. So deeply engrossed, in fact, that he nearly jumped out of his own skin with shock when Mum's face suddenly loomed large behind him in the mirror, yelling: 'FELIX HORATIO STOWE! GET A MOVE ON – WE'RE LATE!'

11

2
THE NEW
BEST FRIEND

Mum was sitting in the car in the drive, revving the engine noisily and shouting out of the window.

'Come ON, Felix! We've got to get Flora!'

'Yeah, hurry up, squirt. Your *girlfriend's* waiting for you,' Merv sneered, emerging from the bathroom at last.

Felix stuck his tongue out at his brother, snatched up his book on apes and shoved his feet into his shoes, slung his coat over one arm and his school bag over the other and raced to the car. He closed the door in time to avoid the smelly sock Merv had hurled from the house.

'Flo is NOT my girlfriend,' he announced,

BOOK ON APES

throwing his bag and coat over the back of the seat into the boot, narrowly missing Dyson. Not that the poor dog seemed to mind. He only snorted slightly before shuffling away from the bag and settling back down to sleep.

'Mmmm,' said Mum distractedly. She was taking Dyson to work with her after dropping Felix and Flo at school. Her office let her do that sort of thing. Dad's didn't, which seemed to annoy Mum rather a lot. Felix thought she should be Over the Moon about working in a place that was so cool they let you take your pets to work. He had personally tried on more than one occasion to convince his teacher, Mr Beasley, to have a Bring-Your-Pet-to-School Day, but he had not yet succeeded.

'We are running an educational establishment, not a zoo, Felix,' Mr Beasley had told him sniffily.

'But having all our different pets to study would be a very Interesting and Educational Thing,' Felix had persisted.

His teacher had not agreed.

This was typical of school. It was all very well when the teachers decided what was Interesting and Educational, but they never did want to take suggestions from the actual people who were there to be educated, i.e. Felix and the other pupils. This was one of the very many reasons why Felix had never had a particularly high opinion of school.

'Mum?' He leaned forward and shouted at Mum above the noise of the radio. 'Mum! I've just had a brilliant idea. School would be a much better place if instead of all those children who are a Waste of Space and Badly Behaved, they let chimpanzees come instead. And maybe spider monkeys and possibly one or two gorillas as well!'

Mum parped the horn as a car pulled out of a side road right in front of her. She muttered something that Felix couldn't hear properly.

'Mum?' he said, more loudly.

'Yes, dear,' she said through gritted teeth. 'I'm

sure the teachers would love that.'

'Well, it would be more exciting than just having Jeff,' Felix went on.

Jeff was kind of a school pet. He was the class mouse in actual fact. But he was a pretty useless sort of pet as he never did anything. Even Hammer did stuff, like put things in his pouches and build nests and sometimes escape. And the thing with Jeff was you were only allowed to play with him when it was your turn to clean out the cage. And that only happened once a month.

Once a month did not really count, in Felix's opinion.

'Oh well, at least Flo understands,' Felix said to himself. He slumped back into his seat and stared out of the window.

School had definitely become a lot more fun once Flo Small arrived on the scene. Before that Felix used to spend break-time alone in a corner of the playground, mostly doing stuff like making 'bug bases' (which were homes for bugs and beetles built from leaves and twigs and stones) or digging holes in the ground to see if he could get to Australia and finally meet a real live kangaroo.

He was doing just this on the very first day that he met Flo. She had walked right up to him and said, 'Are you digging a hole to Australia? If so, you might need some help as it is actually rather a long way from here.' And she had got down on her hands and knees and started digging before Felix had thought of anything to say.

From that day on, Felix and Flo were always together and they didn't care if the Girls Who Giggled teased them or if the Boys Who Played Football called them names.

Felix grinned to himself as he remembered what Flo had said one morning when she'd 'had enough of that lot.'

'You just have to remember that we actually lead far more exciting lives than they do,' she announced loudly. 'Yes,' she said, turning on her heel and shoving her nose in the air. 'We are too busy making Secret Important Plans to take any notice of Them.'

And it was true. Flo and Felix had discovered almost right away that they both knew lots of Incredibly Interesting Facts about wildlife. So they had decided to become officially best friends on that very first day of meeting. And because they lived two streets away from each other it was actually very convenient for them to go round to each other's houses every once in a while – or quite a lot, depending on whether Mum said yes or no.

Flo had been the first person to come round when Felix had found a warty brown toad under a rock near the allotments.

'You are sort of quite cool for a girl,' Felix had told her, watching her hold the toad and stroke it. 'Most girls hate toads.'

'I am not Most Girls,' Flo had said.

She had not been exaggerating. Flo never squealed if a particularly huge and tickly spider climbed up her legs, and she never ran away if a bee made a beeline towards her, and she never said, 'Urgh! Disgusting!' if Felix handed her a centipede or an earthworm. In fact, she was more likely to be the one to have found the centipede or the earthworm in the first place.

She didn't even mind when Dyson came bounding up to her after swimming in the canal and shook water and slobber all over her.

Felix enjoyed spending time with Flo so much, that he thought it would be totally perfect if they could spend even more time together planning their Latest Animal Activity. And that was when he had come up with the suggestion of sharing lifts.

Mum had pulled up outside Flo's house now and Felix had already started bouncing up and down in his seat in anticipation of seeing his friend.

'Mum? Mum! Do you remember when I gave you the Very Good Idea of sharing the school run?' he squealed.

'Mmmm,' said Mum. She was tapping the steering wheel and looking at her watch.

'Can I go and ring the bell?' Felix asked.

'No! You know Flora's mum doesn't like to be hassled. They'll be out in a minute,' Mum said, looking at her watch again. 'Or two . . .'

He had mentioned lift-sharing when his uncle was at their place having supper. Felix had realized long ago that if he wanted to bring up new things it was best to do it while Uncle Zed was there, as he was bound to be on Felix's side about mostly anything.

'Flo and me live really close, you see,' he told his

19

uncle. 'And it would help you, Mum. You don't like the school run,' he added helpfully. 'In fact, you are always saying that if they don't do something about the traffic lights you will personally write to the council and tell them where to stick—'

'Yes, all right, Felix,' Mum said. 'I think you've made your point.'

'But, Mum—'

Uncle Zed quickly cut in above the fight that was threatening to break out. 'Hey, it's a cool idea! Think of the energy you'll save, using one car instead of two, sis? It's putting Green before the Machine. Sweet!'

Uncle Zed was always saying things like this.

'Oh boy,' said Merv, pushing back his chair and slouching off. 'Here we go again: "*You must recycle;*

you must eat mung beans and muesli; you must say 'dude' *after every sentence . . ."'*

'Mervin!' Mum growled. But he had gone.

Zed set to work on Mum after that, persuading her of all the benefits of sharing the school run. Mum was not easily convinced, saying she was 'not sure I could face having Flora Small in the back of the car two or three times a week'.

But Zed was a very good persuader, especially when he mentioned things like 'saving money' and 'saving time', which were things Mum was always worrying about wasting. So in the end Mum had relented, muttering, 'Who would have thought sharing lifts with Flora Small would be a good thing for the planet?'

As a result, Felix was a very happy boy indeed.

3

THE ELEPHANT
IN THE CAR

Good Thing for the planet or not, it had to be said
that Flo could be very (what Mum privately called)
Full of Herself in the mornings. Being Full of
Herself basically consisted of Flo talking non-stop
rubbish from the minute she opened the car door,
according to Mum. And non-stop rubbish was not
something Mum generally found easy to deal with
first thing in the day.

This morning was no exception.

'Did you know that my dad once got attacked
by a Real Live Elephant?' Flo announced, flinging
open the passenger door.

Felix beamed. This was exactly why sharing lifts
with Flo was a brilliant idea.

'Good morning, Flora,' said Mum wearily.

Flo bounced on to the back seat next to Felix and chucked her school bag over her shoulder into the boot, thereby giving Dyson's snoring snout its second near miss of the day.

'It was wild, the elephant,' Flo chattered on, her eyes wide and shining.

Mum turned the radio up suddenly so that the boring man's voice got a bit too loud and meant Flo had to really shout above the news and the traffic reports and the weather and all that yawn-worthy stuff to get Mum to listen to her.

'Yes! A Real Live *Wild* Elephant, right—'

'Strap yourself in, Flora, please,' said Mum.

'How can it have been wild if it attacked your dad?' Felix asked excitedly, getting Bernard the snail out of his pocket and stroking the shell. 'Was he in India or Africa at the time?'

'No, he was in Croydon,' said Flo, pulling the

seat belt out in furious long loops. 'Where his important office work is. WOW!' She started at the sight of Bernard making his way across the back of Felix's hand. 'Is that a—?'

Felix shook his head violently to stop Flo Giving the Game Away to Mum about Bernard and said loudly: 'Go on – what happened?'

Now obviously Flo could handle most bugs and creepy-crawly type things and frogs and toads and whatnot, but it just so happened that she was not all that keen on snails, so she made a face and backed herself into the corner of the car seat, as far away from Bernard as possible. 'We-ell, this Real Live Wild Elephant had escaped from the zoo—'

'Aha! So it wasn't wild then!' Felix cut in, triumphantly waving poor Bernard in the air. The snail zipped back inside his shell in fright. 'It couldn't have been wild if it was in a zoo – animals in zoos are Captivated Animals, you see.'

Flo gave Felix a long hard look with narrowed

eyes and crunched-up eyebrows, and Felix stopped feeling so triumphant. 'So,' he said, a bit nervously, 'what happened next?'

'So the WILD elephant,' said Flo firmly, 'charged at Dad, which was very frightening as he was driving one of those beetle-shaped cars at the time so he couldn't run away. You know the kind I mean. What are they called, those beetle-shaped cars?' Flo called out to Mum.

Mum turned the radio down a tiny bit and said, 'Beetles. *Volkswagen* Beetles, to be precise.'

Flo frowned and then shrugged. 'One of those, yes. He was driving a *Forksvargen*-Beetle-to-be-precise, and then this wild elephant charged at him and stuck his tusks *right through the seat*!' She started kicking the back of Mum's seat in a determined and rhythmical way as if to emphasize her point.

Mum let out a strangled snarl.

Felix gasped. Why did exciting things like this always happen to *Flo's* family? His dad just cycled everywhere. He did not have a car shaped like a beetle, and he had never seen so much as a *badger* on his way to work, let alone a wild elephant. Then again, Felix realized, Dad probably wouldn't tell him even if he *had* seen a wild elephant or a badger. His head was so full of strange work language, such as: 'You've got to push the envelope' and 'I think we should think outside of the box' and 'It's not rocket science', that he wouldn't remember about the elephant or the badger by the time he got home in the evening.

'Wouldn't it be cool to *own* an elephant!' Flo cried suddenly, kicking Mum's seat a bit too hard this time.

'Sit. Still. Flora.' Mum sounded as if she was trying to hold pins in her mouth without dropping them.

'If I was going to own a wild animal,' Felix began, reaching for the book on apes and flicking through the pages, 'I would prefer one of these monkeys that can climb—'

But Flo wasn't listening to Felix. She wasn't listening to Mum either. She was bouncing up and down vigorously, straining at her seat belt as if gravity had suddenly stopped working.

'An *elephant* would be so much more exciting to own than, say, a *snail*,' she said. She fixed Felix with one eyebrow raised in a challenging sort of way.

'Felix!' Mum snapped. 'You haven't brought that snail into the car, have you?'

'Oooo, an elephant!' said Felix enthusiastically. He decided to take Flo's lead – anything if it meant Mum could be diverted from the presence of Bernard. 'It would be totally amazing to have an actual elephant, yes. But how do you think you get to be an Owner of an Elephant – or any wild animal at all?' he added, sticking out his bottom lip thoughtfully. 'That is, unless you are a zookeeper, which I am not.'

'I think you have to prove that you are going to look after it in a responsible way,' Flo said. 'I should ask your Uncle Zed,' she went on. 'He knows everything about all the animals in the world, doesn't he?'

'Mmmm,' said Felix. '*Almost* everything.' Zed hadn't known what to do about the bird Felix had found in the garden which wouldn't fly and wouldn't walk and wouldn't eat the bread and milk he got for it. It had died in the end.

'Of course, it would need tons and tons of green stuff to eat,' continued Flora. 'Does your dad grow enough green stuff for an elephant to eat, d'you think?'

Felix chewed a fingernail and thought it sounded suspiciously as though Flo was having one of her Missions. When Flo had one of her Missions, it usually meant that Felix ended up getting involved in something he couldn't quite remember agreeing to. Like the time Flo had persuaded him that it would be a very Scientific Experiment About Gravity if they put Hammer the hamster at the top of the slide in the garden to see how quickly he would get to the bottom. Everything would probably have been all right if Colin the cat had not noticed and flung himself out of the apple tree in the path of the sliding hamster with the word 'LUNCH' written all over his fangs. Felix had been grounded for a week and Hammer had been so traumatized that the vet had had to give him some special medicine called Sedatives which had Cost the Earth.

Flo stopped bouncing and picked her nose instead. Then she wiped it quietly on the back of Mum's seat while looking at Mum's reflection in the rear-view mirror in an entirely innocent and charming way.

'Hmm. Yes, I think your uncle would know exactly how to get hold of an elephant,' she said. 'And if you looked after it then that would help to protect it from being hunted for its Ivory Bits.'

'It's terribly sad, that hunting thing,' Felix said knowledgeably. 'They use the Ivory Bits for things like drinking horns.'

Flo rolled her eyes. 'Derrrr! Not any more – that was in the Olden-Fashioned Days,' she said in exasperation. 'But they *do* use them for making pianos, you know. I used to have a piano with Ivory Bits for the keyboard – only the white part, obviously. The black keys cannot be made from ivory, as ivory is not black.'

This was so fascinating that Felix had now completely forgotten about the elephant idea. He sat back, his book on apes lying discarded beside him. He had also forgotten about Bernard who had worked his way out of Felix's pocket and on to the edge of the car seat and was making for the door handle.

'So what is the black part of the piano made of?' Felix asked, eyes wide in wonder.

'Oh, sabre-toothed tigers' teeth,' said Flo airily.

'Wow!' said Felix. It never ceased to amaze him how wonderfully wise and full of information his best friend was. He had not even known that sabre-toothed tigers *had* black teeth.

Mum coughed as if something had got stuck in her throat. 'I think you'll find that pianos these days have *plastic* keyboards,' she said, looking at Felix and Flo in the rear-view mirror with a tight-lipped smile.

Flo went a bit red. Then she shrugged and quickly said, 'Well, obviously I know *that*. I don't have that piano any more, anyway. It was an Olden-Fashioned-Day one. I gave it to my worst best friend at my old school . . . So, Felix,' she said, changing the subject in a firm and determined voice, 'what about this elephant then? Shall we get one, or not?'

'No more time to chat,' Mum said, sounding suddenly a lot more cheerful as she pulled into the school car park. 'The bell's about to go – out you get, you two. And careful when you get your bags out the back. We don't want Dyson trying to escape.'

Dyson lifted his head hopefully at the sound of his name.

'Don't forget,' Mum added, raising her voice above Flo who was still rabbiting on about elephants. 'Felix, are you listening? Zed and Silver are picking you up tonight. I'll come and get you from the boat after tea.'

Felix flung open the car door and Bernard took his chance, dropping to the ground and slinking off before he could be pulverized by Felix and Flo as they ran in through the school gates, babbling to each other at top volume just as the bell rang for register.

4
FLO IS
ON A ROLL

Felix could not sit still all of that morning. He could not work out whether he was fizzing with excitement at the prospect of a Real Live Elephant coming to stay, or whether he was full of anxiety and worry about the idea. The more he thought about it, the more he realized it was actually both. An elephant as a pet would mean that life would no longer be boring at home. Even Merv would be impressed and probably leave him alone once he had an elephant by his side.

But then how on earth did anyone get hold of a Real Live Elephant in the first place? Did zookeepers bring them over from Africa on aeroplanes or on ships? And how did you *get* an aeroplane or a ship? Did you have to know someone who owned one, or could you just buy a ticket? He knew that there were planes called jumbo jets. Maybe they were the ones for the elephants.

It was very frustrating. Felix had all these extremely important questions that needed answers, and he was stuck in the classroom learning the nine times table.

He looked across the table at Flo who was busily filling in her maths sheet.

'Flo?' he hissed.

She looked up at him from under her fluffy blonde mop of hair and frowned.

'I need to talk to you about this Elephant Thing,' he whispered.

$9 \times 6 = 42$ ✗

'Felix!' Mr Beasley had magically appeared by his side and was breathing his cheese-'n'-onion breath snortily down Felix's neck. 'You will be staying in at break if you have not finished the worksheet!'

$9 \times 4 = 16$ ✗

$9 \times 9 = 81$ ✓

$9 \times 8 = 99$ ✗

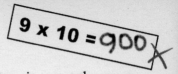
9 x 10 = 900

Felix sighed and started filling in numbers at random.

★

By the time the bell had rung for break, Felix had decided that the whole Elephant Thing was not going to work out. His head was hurting from the nine times table anyway, and he simply didn't have enough brain power left to work out how to get hold of an elephant. He ran into the playground with Flo hot on his heels. Once they were safely by the bug bases and away from the Boys Who Played Football, he turned to face his friend and said, 'About this elephant—'

'Yes, I wanted to talk to you too. I have been thinking about it all morning and I have decided we absolutely must do what we can to Progress This Project immediately,' she said in a posh, TV-newsreader-type voice.

Felix frowned. 'No, I don't agree—'

Flo arched one eyebrow impressively, stopping

Felix in mid-tracks. 'I have actually come up with a brilliant idea which you could say is Foolproof. I was multi-tasking it while I was doing my maths sheet and I have got it all worked out.'

She backed Felix into a corner and, dropping her voice to a hush, told him what they needed was A Plan of Action.

'Last week my dad read a book to me about a man who had travelled to Africa and could talk animal languages and brought animals back from Africa to live in his house. He was called Doctor Dolittle. So you see it must be possible.'

The rumbling feeling Felix had had in his tummy all morning grew stronger. It was panic, he realized. Flo was most definitely On A Roll.

He took a deep breath and said calmly, 'This book could not have been a true-life story if it said that the man could talk animal languages, cos no one in true life can actually do that.'

This was a way of buying Felix a bit of time. He

did secretly think that there probably *were* people who could talk animal languages, because otherwise how did you explain those people on the telly who could get seals to understand exactly what tricks to do in those big swimming pools? And how could people train parrots to talk as well? And once he had seen a sign at the zoo which said 'WOLVES TALK: 2.00 p.m'. (He did wonder why they only spoke at two o'clock in the afternoon, but there were some mysteries in this life which were not worth bothering to solve.)

'Well, it doesn't matter about whether the animal languages bit is true life or not,' Flo said dismissively. 'What I am talking about is getting an elephant.'

'Yes, but, Flo, no one

How many zookeepers does it take to change a light bulb?

Depends how hungry I am

has ever had an elephant as a pet. Not in England anyway. If they did, it would have been on the news,' said Felix. 'And it would never fit inside my house and we only have quite a small garden at the back.' He tried to change the subject altogether. 'Can we talk about apes and monkeys now? Cos I have brought in my book to show you—'

Flo held up her hand. 'I'm sorry, Felix Stowe, but I think you will find that I was talking first.'

Felix rolled his eyes.

'OK,' he said heavily. 'So where do *you* think we would keep it? IF we could get one in the first place,' he added with deep scepticism.

Flo looked up at the sky as if she was talking to someone who had not one single ounce of a brain. 'That would be *your* responsibility, obviously,' she said. 'I absolutely could *not* have it at my place. My mum has only just finished having the garden designed, and Dad has filled the allotment with new plants. And our garage is completely Full to Bursting with simply heaps of stuff. But just imagine!' she said, changing tack hastily. 'If we had our Very Own wild elephant, we could set it on mean people, like Humphrey Darling. He would soon learn his lesson and not flick wet tissues and bogeys at us in RE.'

Felix was worried that he was losing control of the situation far too rapidly. BOGEY Flo was tricky enough to keep up with at the best of times, but today she seemed to be on Planet Janet with the Weirdos. If the elephant lived in his house, how would he get it to school to set it on mean people like Humphrey Darling, for goodness sake? He could hardly just squeeze it into the car without Mum noticing.

'You still haven't said how we are going to *get* this elephant,' Felix said, a bit sulkily.

'Listen,' Flo said, 'you are the one who is always saying that you wish you had a pet that was not boring. And you keep telling me you need a replacement for Jonah.'

Poor Jonah. He had not survived longer than a week. Felix missed him rather a lot considering he was only a goldfish.

'That's true,' Felix said, nodding. 'OK, fine. I'll ask Zed about elephants when he picks me up. It's my birthday soon and he's been asking me what I want as a present . . . Do you want to come back with us tonight and see what he says?'

'Nah,' said Flo. 'I'm going to Millie's.'

Millie was a very pink and girly girl. Felix was about to say as much, but Flo gave him another one of her Looks, so he didn't.

5
THE
FAVOURITE UNCLE

Felix tore out of school at the first sight of his uncle.

'Hey, dude!' Zed cried, throwing his arms round his nephew.

'How do you get hold of a Real Live Extra-Wild Elephant?' said Felix, gasping for breath and struggling to free himself from the monster bear hug.

'Heeey! A joke!' Zed said, slapping Felix on the back. 'What do you reckon, Silvs?' he asked his girlfriend. 'How do you get hold of a Real Life Extra-Wild Elephant?'

'Errr. Like, stick it in the fridge?' Silver asked, twirling one of the long ribbons that trailed from the back of her head like octopus tentacles.

'Yeah! Those jokes always have elephants in

fridges, don't they, Feels?'

'NO!' Felix cried. It was quite frustration-making talking to Zed and Silver sometimes. 'It's not a *joke*! I really entirely mean it – how do you get hold of an extra-wild elephant? To KEEP?'

'OK, OK – less stress!' Zed said, putting a sun-tanned hand on Felix's shoulder. 'You can tell me all about it once we're on the boat.'

But Felix was *desperate* to talk to Zed about the elephant. He was worried that Flo would be asking him for all the details of his conversation with Zed the next morning, so he needed to talk to him – and fast.

'But it's Immensely Important,' Felix said, hopping from foot to foot.

'Feels, man,' said Zed quietly, stooping down and looking deep into his nephew's eyes, 'we have all the time in the world, yeah? Let's save it till we're out of this madhouse.' He nodded in the direction of the hordes of other children streaming out of school towards their parents and carers, all shouting and talking at once.

'All right,' Felix said grudgingly. Zed had a point.

He climbed on to the trailer bike that was attached to the back of Zed's tandem and strapped on the helmet his uncle handed him. This was the way to travel – far better than the car. Zed was up in front, then Silver, and Felix pedalled on the trailer bike behind them. He loved the way the warm spring air went all whooshy around his ears as they sped off down to the tow path. That was the other good thing about the bike – you didn't have to stick to the road, and you didn't get caught in traffic jams.

And there was the whole fascinating world of the canal and the woods lining the tow path in which

Felix could lose himself until they reached the boat.

So even though he was fidgety with impatience he sat back and forced himself to think Happy Thoughts, which ended up being not *that* tricky, as Felix was always happy when he was with his uncle.

'Hey, Feels! Check it out – a kingfisher!' Zed suddenly called over his shoulder. Felix followed the line of Zed's finger and sat up, goggle-eyed.

'Wow,' he breathed. The jewel-like bird zipped along the still, green surface of the canal and dive-bombed after a fish before vanishing into a small hole in the bank.

'Feeding its family. Cool!' said Zed.

Felix found himself wondering yet again how it was possible that Mum and Zed were related. Mum would not have even *seen* the kingfisher, let alone pointed it out to Felix with such relish.

But then Zed was everything that Mum was not. For a start he was a man, although he had long hair (sometimes with beads in). And he had a beard (also sometimes with beads in), which of course Mum did not (although she *did* occasionally wear beads – but they would be round her neck, not anywhere else). And he lived on a boat on the canal instead of in a normal house. And he had a girlfriend called Silver who loved animals as much as Zed and Felix and Flo did. Whereas Mum had a husband called Dad who did not love animals at all, even one tiny bit.

But it wasn't just those kinds of obvious things. Zed never shouted or said, 'We're LATE!' He didn't even wear a watch, as he said, 'Time is, like, a human construct, man. Nature doesn't have a watch – have you noticed? But lambs are still born in the spring and snowdrops still come out at the right season. It's sweet! No need for clockwork.'

Flo loved Uncle Zed almost as much as Felix did.

'You know I've never met anyone with a real-life beard like that one,' Flo told Felix in hushed tones after her first encounter with Zed. 'I mean – is it really real? It's so HUMONGOUS! And all that hair on his head is mega-weird – a bit like snakes or eels. Is that maybe a wig?'

Felix sighed importantly and said, 'Of course it's not a wig. It's his Eco-Hippy Tendencies, Mum says.'

Flo pulled a face. 'What's an Eeeek-o-hippy? Sounds scary and a bit screechy.'

'Not scary – hairy!' Felix said, giggling.

Uncle Zed's real name was Clive, but he had given up that name long ago when he realized that 'the name you're born with is not the name to go forward with into this world' and that it was important to 'take on a name that progressed your journey through life'.

Mum said that was a 'load of cobblers' and that Uncle Zed had got his nickname from the fact that he was well known for taking afternoon naps, or 'catching zeds' as he called it, and that if sleeping was something that progressed your journey through life 'Uncle Zed had progressed enough already to earn himself a free travel pass'.

Felix didn't know what that meant, and he didn't really care. As far as he was concerned, his uncle was the best thing about his family, and that afternoon he had two whole hours with him before Mum had to come and take him home to do homework and tidy his room and other dull and awful things that were Frankly Worse Than Death.

Everything about spending time with Zed was fantastic fun. The boat he lived on (all the time – not just the holidays!) was brilliant, of course. It was painted in a rainbow of patterns and swirls, and was called *Kiboko*. Felix's house was just called 'Number 12', which was hardly a name. *Kiboko* meant 'hippo' in an African language called Swahili. Felix thought it sounded magical and wished that people in England spoke Swahili instead of English. When Felix was still a baby, Zed and Silver had spent two whole years travelling around lots of African countries and they lived in a huge tent that was so big you could actually light a fire in the middle of it and it wouldn't burn down. The tent was called a 'yurt'. Felix didn't know which was cooler – living on a boat on the canal, or living in a yurt in Africa. He decided that maybe living half the year in one and half the year in the other was absolutely the only solution. That way you would get to see all the best animals in the world: moorhens and herons and kingfishers and water voles in the summer in England, and elephants, hippos and giraffes in

Africa the rest of the year.

'We called the boat *Kiboko* to remind us of Africa: hippos are the horses of the river,' Zed had once told him mysteriously. 'That's what the word "hippopotamus" means, man.'

Silver grew plants on the roof of *Kiboko* – herbs and pots of chrysanthemums and even pumpkins in the autumn – and there were two black and white cats, Yin and Yang, who slept on the patchwork quilt on the bed. They were soft and cuddly cats who spent most of their lives sleeping. (Not like Colin who spent most of his life sticking his claws into anything that got in his way.) Best of all there was always a huge biscuit tin in the tiny galley kitchen, full of chocolate biscuits. Felix couldn't for the life of him think of a sensible reason why the whole world didn't live exactly as Zed and Silver did.

The tandem passed a couple of moored boats and a chicken run and approached the familiar little stone bridge near where *Kiboko* was secured.

'Here we are.' Zed chained the bike up alongside the boat and waved cheerily to his neighbour who was just taking his own boat back to its mooring.

Felix smiled. The calm of the water, the birdsong in the air and the sight of the brightly coloured boats reassured him. A proud mother duck was parading her new family of

ducklings on the water right alongside *Kiboko*. This was a world where anything was possible – where the Normal Rules did not apply. Silver hopped on board to put the kettle on the stove and get the biscuit tin out. The sun was beaming, and the cats were stretched out on the roof on their backs, for all the world as if they were trying to get a tan.

'I wish this was my house,' Felix said, climbing up next to the cats, and flopping down on to his back. It was so warm up there! Yin raised his head and blinked at Felix, stretched, purred briefly and went back to sleep.

Zed stuck his head out of the galley window and said in a mock-stern voice, 'Hey, I've told you before: *Kiboko*'s not a house, man. Houses are boxes that hold us in and keep us back. Not cool.'

Felix peeped over the side at his uncle. 'So, back to this elephant then,' he said. He was not going to let Zed get distracted and start talking about Living it Green.

Zed grinned, and said, 'Hit me with it.'

'Hit you with what?' Felix asked, puzzled.

'The elephant idea!' Zed said. 'What's the grand plan, man?'

6
ADOPTING AN ELEPHANT

Felix took a deep breath and said: 'We-ll . . . You know it's my birthday really soon?' He looked down at Yin who was purring like a jet plane about to take off, and tickled him under the chin. Silver came out of the galley with two huge chipped mugs of sweet peppermint tea and handed one to Zed.

'Yeah!' said Zed. 'Are you going to have, like, a totally massive party with jelly beans and pass the parcel and stuff? Awesome!'

Silver caught Felix's eye and smiled in a knowing way that Felix was sure meant, 'I love Zed, but sometimes he has no idea, does he?'

'Er, we don't have parties like that any more,' said Felix, squirming. He didn't want Zed to think he was being rude.

'Oh,' said Zed, crestfallen.

Silver put a hand on his arm. 'So what *are* you going to do, Feels?' she asked.

'Well, Mum said I could have a Special Birthday Outing to a place I could choose. So I said I wanted to go to Africa like you did, but she said it had to be in this country and somewhere we could get to in less than an hour,' Felix said solemnly.

Silver bit her lip and nodded.

'So,' Felix went on, 'I said if it couldn't be Africa it did have to be somewhere that had something to do with animals, and then Dad suggested that Shortfleet safari place that's on the telly. You know, where they film that *Safari Park Live* programme with Kitty Bumble and Tim Bogel and they talk about the lions and giraffes and stuff?'

Silver nodded again.

'So Mum said yes, and I'm asking Flo to come too,' Felix finished.

Zed had perked up at the mention of the safari park. His eyes were shining. 'Shortfleet? Man, that place is cool! They are so into conservationism there — you know, like, looking after endangered species? And the guy who owns it — Lord Basin — he's a dude. He lived in Kenya years ago. I've always wanted to meet the guy . . . Hey! Any chance I could get an invite?'

'Course!' said Felix.

'Awesome! It's meant to be, like, massive — a palace! And the Lord dude, he has wild animals roaming around — even inside. And the walls are decorated with mega stuff he's brought back from his travels. And he wears clothes that are way cool—'

'Yes, erm, talking of that "conversationism" stuff, back to my elephant question,' Felix cut in.

'Like I said: hit me with it.' Zed drained his tea in one gulp and slammed the mug down on the roof of the boat. Yin leaped up from Felix's lap, his startled eyes popping out of his chequerboard face, and scarpered inside to safety.

Felix scrunched his eyes up tight and took a deep breath. Then he said, very quickly: 'Flo thinks we should get an elephant of our own to look after. Did you know that people steal elephants and kill them for the Ivory Bits to make pianos and stuff? It's horrid and—'

'Hold it!' Zed butted in, holding up one hand like a traffic policeman. 'Let me get this straight – you want an *elephant*? Like, for *real*?'

Felix nodded. 'Yes.'

Zed looked at Silver and then looked back to Felix. He let his hand fall back down to his side, his jaw dropped and his eyes popped open so that Felix could see all the white around the blue. Felix leaned back on his arms, feeling a bit worried about what Zed would do next. Then his uncle slapped his thighs and shouted, 'An elephant as a pet! Whooo-hoooo! Crazy, man! A JUMBO

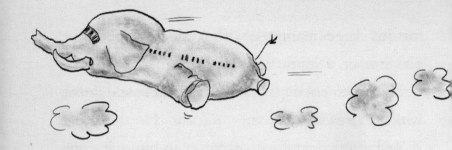

PET! Like a jumbo JET – geddit?' He roared with laughter. 'You kill me!'

Felix frowned. He didn't like being laughed at. Not when he had something so serious to talk about.

Silver looked at Zed and shook her head.

Zed said, 'What?' Then he saw the expression on his nephew's face and sobered up. 'Sorry,' he said, 'but I'm still not quite following what you're saying. You don't want *me* to get you an elephant? As in a huge grey pachyderm with tusks and a trunk?'

'Ye-es,' said Felix. 'Well, it has tusks and a trunk, anyway. But I don't know about any packy-wotsit.'

Silver chuckled. 'A pachyderm – it's the name

for any large mammal with a thick skin – like a rhino, or a hippo? It comes from the Ancient Greek words *pakhus*, which means thick, and *derma*, which means skin.'

Zed grinned and hugged Silver to him with one arm. 'The girl knows what she's talking about.'

Felix chewed his bottom lip. 'Did they have elephants in Ancient Greek times then?' he asked.

'Man, elephants are an ancient species,' Zed said, looking suddenly grave. 'That's why it is so seriously bad that humankind has not looked after them.'

'That's exactly why Flo thinks we should get one,' Felix said enthusiastically. He jumped off the roof, clutching the biscuit tin with both hands, and landed heavily in front of Zed and Silver, which made the boat rock a bit.

'Steady!' said Silver, as she grabbed a mug to stop it falling.

But Felix was waving his arms about chaotically.

'Flo said you would know how to get an elephant because you know Nearly Everything About Animals and you've lived in Africa in a yurt. I can't ask Dad as he's too stressed about his meetings and stuff, and I can't ask Mum because she already threw a wobbly when I asked her if I could have some chickens or ferrets.'

Silver raised one pierced eyebrow. 'Chickens and ferrets, eh?' she said, placing the mug gingerly back on the water tank.

Felix carried on talking and squeezed into the space between Zed and Silver, forcing Silver to save the mug again from disaster. 'Yes. But obviously not together, as the ferrets would probably eat the chickens and that would be no good as I want the chickens to live so that I can have their eggs,' he explained seriously. 'You remember me asking

Mum about the chickens, don't you, Zed?'

Zed was staring out across the canal in a dream. 'Eh? Chickens? Oh yeah, my sis is not a bird–dude, dude,' he explained to Silver. 'She, like, hates all the pecking and clucking and stuff? And she thinks they stink.'

Felix nodded again. 'But they don't – and keeping them is so easy and cheap cos they can live off potato peelings and rubbishy food that humans don't eat. I looked it all up on the Internet and you can buy a chicken for one pound from the RSPCA.'

Zed chuckled. 'Man, you are crazy. Shame you can't get an elephant from the RSPCA!'

'The RSPCA only has animals from *this* country,' Felix explained patiently through a mouthful of chocolate crumbs.

'Wait! I've had a cool idea,' Silver cried. Her bangles jingled madly as she held the mug in mid-air and pointed it straight at Felix. 'There *is* a way you can get an elephant, Feels! Zed and I can do it for you as a birthday present, *and* you'll be helping to protect it too.'

Zed shot Silver an extremely worried look as if she had suddenly gone completely mad. He shifted slightly. 'Silvs?' he said quietly, a questioning note in his voice. 'I don't think it's cool to buy any kind of animal off the Internet as a birthday present, that's *way* far out. It's probably not even legal—'

'Hey, chill! You don't BUY them,' said Silver, giggling. 'You ADOPT them.'

Zed looked at her quizzically for a full beat and then threw back his dreads and howled with glee. 'Man, of course! That *is* an awesome idea. Yeah, I'll do that for you, no worries, Felix. Silvs, you're a genius.'

Silver grinned and bowed her head, accepting the compliment.

Felix was confused. 'How can you do this adopting thing?'

Silver picked up her mug and took a long and satisfying slurp. 'You just need to look up one of the charities on the Internet and choose the animal you want to help protect, and then you send the charity money. Then the charity sends you an email back saying you've adopted the animal. You get information packs, newsletters and—'

But Felix wasn't interested in the details. 'Yippeeeee!' he shouted, bouncing up and down on the water tank. 'Flo will be soooo excited! And I've been *desperate* for a really interesting animal to look after for ages. Besides, I do sort of need a replacement for Jonah.'

'Jonah?' Zed asked.

'You remember Jonah,' said Felix. 'My goldfish.'

'You *must* remember Jonah,' said Silver mischievously. 'He's the little guy who went for a white-knuckle ride and didn't survive.'

'No he didn't,' said Felix. 'Fish don't have

knuckles. Anyway what happened was I had to put him in the loo while I cleaned out the tank cos Merv was using the basin to dye his hair again, and then I got distracted because I saw a woodpecker out of the window, so I went to get my binoculars, and when I came back Jonah was swishing down the loo and it was too late to get him back. I made Dad go and look in the pipes to see if he could find Jonah, but it was no good. We put a cross in the garden so we would remember him forever. It was really sad.'

'Like I said – white-knuckle ride,' said Silver, squeaking a bit.

'Oh, you didn't like FLUSH IT, did you?' squawked Zed.

'No, I did not!' cried Felix indignantly. And then, quietly: 'Merv did.'

'Man!' yelped Zed, clutching his sides. 'He is one crazy guy . . . OK,' he said, putting on a more serious face. 'So you need a pet to replace Jonah and shake life up a bit in the Stowe household.'

'Exactly!' said Felix enthusiastically.

Zed leaned over the side of *Kiboko* and threw the dregs of his peppermint tea into the canal. Felix wondered if all the people who lived on the boats drank peppermint tea and chucked it into the river, and that, if they did, that was possibly why the water was so green and murky.

'There's just one, like, *miniscule* kind of nano-problem about this adopting thing?' Zed was saying. 'And that is, I, er, I don't have a computer.'

'Why not?' Felix asked, leaping up and spinning round and almost losing his balance. He wheeled his arms round and round to stop himself falling into the water and then did a kung-fu kind of chop in the air to cover up for the fact that he looked like a bit of a doofus.

Zed roared with laughter, and cried, 'Hey! Watch out – you'll scare the ducks, man!'

Felix felt his ears go hot. Then he said a

little crossly, 'Anyway, I thought you *did* have a computer. I thought that Mum gave you her old laptop because she was going to throw it away, and you said that she couldn't do that because it would go straight into the landfill place where they bury all the rubbish. And then you said you would take it from her and Reuse or Recycle it so that it didn't end up ruining the atmosphere with bad chemicals and things.'

Zed was always telling Felix how important it was to Reduce and Reuse and Recycle. He also said it was important not to own very much stuff, which apparently included not having a telly. Felix thought this was going a bit too far. He could see the point of Reusing, particularly when it came to wearing the same pair of socks over and over again. And he was pretty good at Recycling, especially yoghurt cartons. They made really good caterpillar homes.

He had never understood

what Reducing was, though. Maybe there was a clever scientific way of shrinking things to an almost invisible size, so that they didn't take up too much room on the planet. If so, Felix thought Merv should put himself forward for it.

'Yeah well, I'm really sorry, Feels,' Zed was mumbling, 'but reusing was not going to work with that computer. Your mum was not fibbing when she said that it was broken. I tried everything, man – I even gave it to Piggy – you know, my mate who's cool with technology and that? But even he couldn't do anything with it.'

'So you threw it away into the landfill place after all?' Felix said, eyes wide with outrage.

'No! No!' Zed protested. 'If you can't reuse, *recycle*, remember? I took it to this place in town where they take computers to pieces

and recycle what's inside them and make them into other things.'

'Other computers?' Felix asked, his eyes lighting up.

'Er – I guess so,' Zed muttered, inspecting the big toe on his right foot.

'So can we go there and ask them to make us a new one out of the Bits and Bobs from the old one then? That would be like a second-hand computer, wouldn't it? Like from one of those shops for charity where you take in your old clothes and toys and you can spend your pocket money on *new* clothes and toys except that it's much cheaper than what your own *old* stuff really cost when it was new?' Felix was getting really excited now. He could just see himself walking into this place in town and giving them all his pocket money (he had £9.76 now, which was a Total Fortune and would be bound to impress them in the shop) and walking out with his very own laptop!

Zed looked up at Felix through his stringy hair and said, 'No, mate. Sorry. It's all in pieces now and that's that. No more computer. *Finito. Nada. Kaputt.*'

'What?' said Felix, shaking his head. Was Zed speaking Swahili again? But even though he didn't understand some of the words he knew what Zed was telling him. 'Never mind,' he said brightly. 'We can use the computer at my place. You're picking me up tomorrow with Flo, aren't you? You can go on the Internet at my house then. We'll have loads of time to look up everything before Mum gets home!'

Zed nodded slowly. 'Sounds like a plan. OK. I'll tell your mum I'll cook supper tomorrow.'

Felix's face split into the cheesiest grin ever to be seen on anything that wasn't made of cheese. 'Yay!' he shouted, punching the air with his fist.

7

FLO'S
NEW IDEA

'Zed said "yes"!' Felix whispered to Flo.

It was the next morning and Mrs Small was doing the school run. He didn't want her hearing about the elephant as she would be bound to try and Put A Stop to it. Mums always did try and Put A Stop to anything fun or exciting in life.

'What?' Flo shouted. She had her headphones on because she was trying to get to Level 5 on her favourite game, Animal World, where the tortoise lets you buy a twirly umbrella to match the curtains in your house.

Mrs Small hated Animal World 'with a passion'. She said it was a 'waste of time' and that Flo became 'so impossible to live with' when she played it that Mrs Small frequently said she felt as if she had 'frankly lost the will to live'. Felix just thought it was boring cos he couldn't play it with her, and the animals in the game did not behave like real live animals, because they had hats and umbrellas and houses, and Felix did not approve of such nonsense.

He tried once more to compete with Animal World for Flo's attention by lifting one of the earpieces and yelling right into Flo's ear, 'Zed said "YES"!'

'Hey!' Flo yelled back, leaping in her seat and glaring accusingly at Felix. 'Whaddayoudo that for?'

Felix pointed to Flo's ears and mimed taking off the headphones.

'Flora Small, for goodness sake stop screeching like that – oh, you haven't brought that *awful* game with you? Honestly, I feel as if I'm losing the will—'

'ALL RIGHT!' Flo said to Felix crossly. She

yanked off the headphones. She had not heard a word her mum had said, which Felix thought was just as well, as he didn't enjoy the journey to school with Flo and her mum bickering. Flo seemed to actually *like* a good fight, Felix had discovered. Mrs Small would say, 'It's a bit nippy today,' and even if Flo's teeth were chattering and the tip of her nose was turning blue, she would say, 'No it's not. The sun is shining.'

'So what is more important than Level Five then?' Flo said, turning on Felix moodily.

Felix ignored the sulky tone and announced, 'Zed said he's going to adopt me an elephant!'

Flo's moodiness turned to hyper-excitedness in the blink of a second. 'OH! That is fanterabulacious!' she cried. 'What kind of elephant? African or Indian?'

'African,' Felix said firmly. 'Ears are important when it comes to elephants, and everyone knows that African ones have the biggest. Anyway, Zed lived in Africa, so he'll know all about how to feed it and so on.'

'Good,' Flo said, nodding seriously. 'And will it be fully grown or still kind of a baby? Babies don't have tusks, you know.'

Felix got a tiny bit irritated when he realized that he hadn't thought through many of the details. 'I *know* babies don't have tusks,' he said, and then to Mrs Small: 'Can Flo come round for tea tonight to do Research on Elephants?'

'That sounds lovely, dear,' she replied. 'Now, grab your bags – we're here.'

There was still time before registration as they were early for once, so Felix and Flo raced into the playground to the bench where they began to plan for the arrival of the elephant in earnest.

'So, first of all, we need to write it all down,' said Flo, rummaging in her book bag for a pencil and a special-looking sparkly notebook.

Felix eyed the notebook suspiciously. 'I thought you didn't like sparkly things that were girly?' he asked her.

Flo blushed a bit and snapped, 'It's not mine, OK? I kind of borrowed it from Millie yesterday.'

Felix shrugged. 'OK.'

Flo started scribbling furiously on one of the pink pages. 'El-e-fants and Addopshun' she wrote and then turned to Felix excitedly. 'So, what are you going to call it? Will it be a boy or a girl?'

Felix rolled his eyes. 'Duuuuuh! It will already *have* a name, won't it?'

'That's not fair!' Flo protested. 'If it's going to be *our* elephant, *we* should get a chance to name it!'

'Look,' Felix replied extra-patiently, 'if *you* were a baby and *you* were adopted, then your *real* mum would have given you a name and so your *adopted* mum would have to keep calling you that *same* name, otherwise you would get confused.'

'You know nothing about adoption,' said Flo,

tutting. 'If you are a baby, then you don't know your name yet, so you *can* be called another name, actually, and it won't matter. Anyway,' she added, a note of triumph entering her voice, 'elephants don't understand human language, so you can call them anything you like.'

Felix thought that for once he might get really quite annoyed with Flo. He was about to say so when Flo's pink friend from the day before walked up and said, 'Flora Small, that is MY notebook you are writing in, I think you will *find*.'

'OH WELL I'm so *sorry*, Millie Hampton, but I think *you* will find that *you* said *I* could *borrow* it, and so *that* is what I am doing,' said Flo, standing up and putting her hands on her hips in a quite impressively scary manner. Felix shrank back into the bench a bit, just in case.

Millie Hampton raised her eyebrows. 'And what is so important that you need to write it all down in MY notebook?' she asked.

Flo narrowed her eyes and said, 'Not that it is *actually* any of your *business*, I think you'll find, but Felix and I are planning to open a zoo, *actually*.'

Felix made a small squeaky sound. He wasn't quite sure where it had come from, but it was the only noise he seemed capable of making in response to such an outrageous claim. A *zoo*? What on earth was she talking about?

'Yes,' Flo said. 'We are starting with an elephant, which Felix is adopting for an extra-special birthday present, and once that has settled into its New Environment, we will move on to bigger and better things such as bears and giraffes. (But obviously not together as the bear would probably eat the giraffe and that would not be very good news for the giraffe.)'

Felix had stopped breathing. This was unbelievable. He knew that Flo had always enjoyed telling Tall Stories, as Mum called them – like the time she told Felix that her dad was in hospital and only had days to live, but actually he was in Swindon teaching a computer skills course.

Anyway, Felix was ninety-nine point nine per cent certain that Flo had *not* got him to agree to this new zoo idea. Flo had mentioned about possibly adopting a few monkeys once the elephant had settled in, but no one had ever said anything about bears or giraffes. Bears and giraffes were slightly harder to hide in a house than an elephant, surely?

'A zoo? Coolio McSquoolio!' Millie said. 'Will you get any flamingos? I love flamingos! They're so PINK!' And she ran off squealing and flapping her arms, telling anyone who could be bothered to listen that she was a flamingo.

Flo rolled her eyes and blew out through her nose, sending a fleck of snot flying out, Felix noticed, though he decided now was not the time to mention this.

'*She* is a Waste of Space.' Flo grimaced.

'But I thought you went to her house yesterday?' Felix pointed out.

'So?' said Flo. 'Doesn't mean I have to like her *today*, for heaven's sake. Now, what do you think about my new idea?'

Luckily Felix was what is called Saved by the Bell – in other words, he didn't have to think of an answer straight away or try to understand what he had just been told about the complicated rules of girls' friendships, because the bell for registration rang.

Felix found his mind wandering during the first lesson, which was geography. Felix was not a Big Fan of geography. He could not see the point of knowing about gorges and rainfall and evaporation. When would he ever need to know about evaporation, for goodness sake? All evaporation was good for was making steam, and when did a human need steam in the course of a normal day?

Felix began staring out of the window at the new, fresh, green leaves on the beech tree in the playground. He loved new beech leaves: they were soft and furry like newborn baby mice. He pondered for a while on the marvels of New Life and from there his mind wandered to tiny elephants being born, and before he knew it he was thinking about what Flo had said to Millie about the zoo.

We can't have a zoo, he thought. In fact, I'm really not at all sure even about adopting an elephant, now that I come to think of it.

He went round and round in circles in his head, fretting and sweating. How was he going to get out of this? Flo was going to be so cross with him if he told her he'd changed his mind.

He put his head in his hands and groaned aloud.

'Felix STOWE!' Mr Beasley shouted.

Felix jumped and knocked his table's pot of crayons flying. 'Er – evaporation?' he twittered, thinking he'd missed a question.

'*What?*' Mr Beasley barked. 'I asked you how your diagram of the water cycle was coming along!'

'Fine, fine,' Felix answered, shifting his eyes sneakily sideways at Flo's exercise book, on which was a beautiful picture, all coloured in with the arrows pointing the right way and everything.

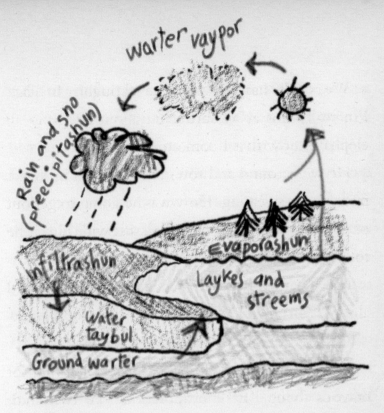

He scrabbled to pick up a blue crayon from the spilt pot and started scribbling furiously to try to persuade his teacher that he was in fact colouring in a blue lake. Mr Beasley sighed heavily and crossed his arms and walked to the other side of the classroom to see how some others were getting on.

'Flo, are you serious about the zoo?' Felix

whispered, leaning towards Flo so that the teacher wouldn't see he was talking.

'OK, well, maybe not an *actual* zoo,' she said quietly. 'I'm not sure how you get the cages and stuff for that. But maybe we could just get a few more animals that need looking after and then we could let them free into the wild when they are ready. What about that?'

Felix shrugged. 'Dunno,' he said. His mind was full of images of adopted elephants being let loose on to the housing estate where he lived. But hopefully that didn't count as The Wild. At least Flo had backtracked a bit on the zoo idea, though.

But Flo had no intention of backtracking. Instead she had started drawing elaborate pictures of animals on her water-cycle diagram. 'Elephants need green stuff to eat, so we will have to keep it in *your* garden,' she said. 'And say we had a few seals to keep the elephant company . . . they would need water to swim in. Well, I've got a pond at home, don't forget.'

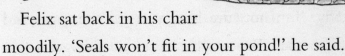

Felix sat back in his chair moodily. 'Seals won't fit in your pond!' he said.

'That is the only correct statement you've made so far this morning, Felix Stowe.' Mr Beasley was standing over him, shaking his head in disbelief at the scribbly blue blob in Felix's geography exercise book. 'Now – I think you'll be staying in at break-time to finish your diagram, won't you?'

Felix should have been relieved to hear the bell go at the end of the day. Break-time had been the worst ever with Mr Beasley breathing his cheese-'n'-onion breath down Felix's neck. And lunchtime had been pretty bad, with Flo wittering on to Felix about the zoo, which was growing vaster by the minute. When she started talking in great detail about the Marmoset Enclosure in Felix's bathroom, he raised his voice and said in a panic, 'FLO! Flo . . . I was thinking about the elephant—'

But it was no good – she simply raised her voice higher and talked right over him.

'I KNOW! I can't STOP thinking about it! It's sooooo exciting!'

'Yeah, erm – maybe it would be more exciting if we just *visited* one—'

'You're right. We should visit one *first*, so we know what to expect.'

The conversation had gone from Downright Difficult to Completely Impossible. Felix miserably decided that he did not know how to get out of the hole he was now in. Flo was dead set on the elephant, and nothing short of an earthquake or some other totally major event was going to distract her or change her mind.

8

FELIX GOES
FOR PLAN B

Zed and Silver were waiting for Flo and Felix outside school. They had each brought a bike with its own trailer so that Felix could pedal behind Zed, and Flo could pedal behind Silver. The cats had come along for the ride too. Yin was in Silver's basket and Yang was in Zed's.

'Oooh, they are just so cuuuuuute!' cooed Flo, in what Felix thought was quite a girly way.

People stared at them and waved as they went past and commented on the cats, who occasionally woke and stretched and peeked over the edge of the baskets. Felix felt altogether rather Special and Important, which cheered him up a bit after the Very Uncomfortable Day he had just had.

Flo quickly tired of the whole bike ride thing, though.

'I wish people would stop waving and calling out,' she shouted grumpily after about the hundredth passer-by had said, 'Hellooooo!'

'Why?' Silver asked.

'It's embarrassing when I can't wave back, cos I'm concentrating so extra-hard on not falling off,' Flo moaned. 'And my hair is flicking into my mouth when I speak, so I can't shout "hello" back at them,' she added, through a mouthful of blonde fluff.

Flo's hair was, even on a normal, unwashed day, the bounciest, curliest, ringlet-iest hair Felix had ever seen on a human being. It reminded him of a poodle's fur, except that it was shinier and didn't smell doggy.

Felix loved it. He often found himself thinking

84

that he would like to take one of the curls of her hair and wind it round and round his finger the opposite way from the curl to see if it would straighten out, like you can with those curly ribbons you get on presents at Christmas. He was sure that if he had hair as fascinating as Flo's he would play with it all the time and possibly hide useful things in it like spare pencils and rubbers and spiders and stuff. Maybe even hamsters as well. You could take Hammer around with you everywhere for a Total Eternity if you had hair like that. No one would ever know.

But even Felix could see the downside to having Flo's hair when you were on a windy bike ride. Poor Flo looked like a yeti by the time they reached Felix's house. (Not that Felix had ever seen a yeti in real life, but he was sure it would look like Flo did at that moment in time.) Her hair had gone into a wild manic frizz-ball so that it was not just sticking out in its usual triangly way, but was now sticking bolt upright as well as out. She actually looked a bit like a dandelion clock too, except her hair was yellow and not white, thought Felix, as he got off the trailer bike and helped Zed lock it up down the side of the house.

'Hello, everyone!' trilled Mum, opening the door to greet them. 'Is that you hiding under there, Flora?' she asked.

This was a bit mean, Felix thought, as it was quite obvious Flo was Suffering a Great Deal already.

Flo scowled from under her yellow birds' nest and puffed at her fluffy fringe.

Felix was annoyed that Mum was home early. He had rather been hoping that he and Zed and Flo could have had a Moment's Peace together before she arrived on the scene.

'So you're doing a project on elephants at school,

Felix tells me?' Mum said.

'No— I mean, *yes* absolutely that is correct!' said Flo.

Felix's heart was fluttering so hard it hurt. It was bad enough being worried about hiding an elephant in the house without Flo giving the game away.

'Riiiight,' said Mum. 'Well, you'd better lock your bike up, Silver, and I'll help with those bags of food.'

'Thanks, Marge,' said Silver. She flicked her tentacles of hair over one shoulder and heaved her bike down the side of the house while Zed got the food out of the bike panniers.

'Oh, Clive. You haven't brought the cats with you?' Mum moaned, catching sight of Yin's little face peering over the side of Silver's basket.

Zed winced. He didn't like Mum calling him Clive, even though that was his real name.

'Listen, sis – less stress, OK? It's cool with the

cats. They won't be any bother,' Zed said.

'But if Colin sees them—' Mum started.

'Colin won't see them if they stay in the baskets,' Silver said, laying a calming hand on Mum's arm. 'Now, you were going to help me carry this lot in,' she said, pointing to the food.

Mum sighed and picked up some bags.

Once inside the house, Flo made a beeline for Hammer's cage, as ever, and started fussing over him and calling him 'the cleverest little cutie-pie in the world' because he could sit up on his hind legs and she thought he was begging for food when he did this. Felix thought it was because it was the only way he could see what was going on outside his cage.

Dyson jumped up and licked Zed and tried to get inside the food bags.

Colin meanwhile sat on the bottom stair in the hall and glared at all of them as if they had invaded his private sanctuary and ruined his peace and quiet. Which, in a way, they had.

'What's on the menu, Clive?' Mum asked, kicking her shoes off.

'We're having beany-cheese crunch,' said Zed. 'Cool with that?'

Mum shrugged. 'It could be cheesy-bean crunch, or crunchy-bean cheese,' she said. 'I don't really mind, as long as someone else is cooking it.'

'There's not any actual real *beans* in it, is there?' asked Flo, narrowing her eyes suspiciously. Hammer was running up and down her arm wildly as she spoke. 'Only I am not Keen On Beans of any kind. In fact, even thinking about beans can actually make me sick. Like this,' she added, clutching her throat with a free hand and rasping and choking.

Hammer went berserk at the noise and tried to run up Flo's sleeve.

'Yeek!' screamed Flo, grabbing the poor hamster and holding on to him a bit too tightly.

'Flo!' cried Felix. 'Put Hammer back in his cage.'

'I think I might, yes,' said Flo, hastily dropping Hammer in and shutting the door firmly.

Mum was rolling her eyes and pursing her lips which was something she often did, and seemed to do more and more when Flo was around. 'Flora, I don't think it's very polite of you to comment on someone else's cooking like that. Particularly when you are a guest and Clive has been very kind—'

Zed cut in quickly to avoid a stand-off between Mum and Flo: 'Oh, these beans won't make you sick,' he said confidently. 'They're *magic* beans.'

Flo turned her award-winning scowl on Zed and said sneerily, 'Yeah, right.' Her eyes were narrowed so much that they were just slits.

But they popped wide open again when Silver lifted up a wodge of Flo's blonde curls and whispered in her ear, 'Chocolate brownies and strawberries for afters. Awesome or what?'

Flo beamed. Even she did not have an answer to that.

'OK,' said Flo. 'I'll help with the tea. Felix, you and Zed can start the research and then I'll come and see what you have done.'

Felix thought this was a bit Typical of Flo, leaving the actual work part of things to him. But he very quietly breathed a huge sigh of relief as Flo disappeared with Silver and Mum. He was glad of the chance to be alone with Zed: he had to talk to him about this elephant business in private. It was Doing His Head In, as Merv would say.

'So, you ready, dude?' Zed asked him, making his way into the study where Mum's computer was. He pulled out the swivelly chair and leaned down to switch on the computer. 'We'll do the Google thing first, yeah?' he said, grinning at Felix.

Felix gave his uncle a sideways glance and shuffled from foot to foot.

Zed put his head on one side. 'What's up?' he asked.

Felix stared at the floor and concentrated hard on not panicking. The thumping in his chest had reached a level of such painfulness that he wondered if it might explode in a minute.

'Come on, dude, I know something's up – tell me!' Zed insisted, putting a large warm hand on Felix's shoulder.

Felix chewed his lip. He could not meet Zed's eye.

How am I going to say this? he thought.

Then: 'I – Idon'twantyoutoadoptmeanelephant!' It all came out in a rush before he could think of a better way of putting it.

'You *don't* want me to?' Zed repeated. 'Well, that's cool. We can look at other animals instead if you like.'

Felix felt a warm rush of affection for his uncle. Why had he been so worried about talking to Zed? Nothing was ever complicated with Zed. He didn't get suspicious and say, 'What are you up to?'

He just asked a question and, when you gave him an answer, he accepted it and that was that. Felix suddenly knew everything was going to be OK. He took a deep breath and went on: 'There's another thing I'm rather worried about too, now I come to think of it.'

'What's that?'

'I don't think we should tell Mum about any kind of Actual Adoption as she's not likely to be keen what with Dyson and Colin and Hammer and all the cleaning out she says she has to do,' Felix said.

'OK,' said Zed slowly, swinging round on the chair to face the computer screen. 'But tell me,' he went on, 'why the change of plan about the elephant, man?'

Felix hoisted himself up on to the desk and swung his legs awkwardly. 'I just think they're too big,' he said.

'But that's no problem, is it?' Zed said, looking puzzled.

'Well, I think it *is* a problem really,' Felix said. 'I did try last night to see how big a Real Live Elephant would be – I started to build one using those cardboard boxes Dad has been keeping in the shed – but once I had built one leg there was no more room. I didn't even get to do the body. And then there's those ears and the trunk. Those beasts are utterly ginormous!'

'Wow, that's a cool idea – building a cardboard elephant!' Zed grinned. 'I still don't get what the problem is, though.'

Felix sighed. Why didn't Zed understand? He had been to Africa – he *knew* how big elephants were. He must see that there was no room for one in Felix's house, and it certainly was not possible to *hide* one anywhere. Felix's heart had started up again. He blinked and swallowed hard.

Zed was frowning at him. 'You OK, man? You've gone kind of green.'

Felix nodded and gulped in some air. 'Fine,' he croaked.

Zed shook his head and turned to face the screen. He clicked on the Internet icon. 'Hey, no worries. If you've changed your mind, it's no sweat to me. Let's have a look at the WWF site. There are, like, heaps of other animals that need help.'

Felix turned his head so he could see the screen better.

It's OK, he told himself. Maybe I can get Zed to adopt me a monkey after all. Cos a monkey is bound not to be so much work as an elephant, he reasoned, and definitely not as big. And I already know loads about monkeys and what they like to eat and stuff. And then when I tell Flo I don't want an elephant any more I can at least say I've chosen something else instead. In fact, he thought, brightening slightly, I might be able to say, 'We are getting monkeys this time as they are the best animals to start a zoo with. We can get the elephant later.' She might forget all about the elephant and the zoo once we have the monkeys, he thought hopefully.

But then he suddenly remembered the look of determination on Flo's face when she had first thought of the whole idea. He shivered. He did not want to make Flo angry: she was his best friend ever, and if she got cross with him he would have to go back to digging holes to Australia on his own at break-time.

'Look at this!' Zed cried, interrupting his miserable thoughts. His uncle was pointing at the screen excitedly. 'There's tigers and polar bears and rhinos—'

'Anything smaller?' Felix asked, anxiously scanning the list.

'Listen, if it's the cost you're worried about . . .' Zed began, looking at Felix's concerned expression.

'No – not that,' Felix said. 'I just think, well, adopting a smaller animal would be easier.'

Zed laughed and shook his head. 'You kill me, man! Anyone would think you were going to invite it to live with you right here!'

Felix frowned. Was this one of Zed's jokes maybe? Felix had always had trouble working out when Zed was joking and when he wasn't. Like the time Zed told Felix that bananas grew in the ground like potatoes. Felix loved bananas, so he'd taken one from the fruit bowl and dug a hole in the garden and planted the banana in the  hope that he'd soon have his very own banana plant right outside the back door. When he'd told his uncle what he'd done, Zed had laughed so much that he had keeled over on to the floor. Felix went red at the memory. Yes, he decided, his uncle was teasing him again. Of course he was going to invite the animal to 'live right here' – where else would it go?

'So, what other animals are there, then?' Felix asked.

'What about gorillas?' Zed asked.

Felix twisted his mouth to one side thoughtfully. 'Hmm,' he said, 'gorillas are cool. In fact, it says in my book on apes that gorillas are very intelligent—'

'Whoa – this is one heavy guy!' said Zed, who had been clicking his way through a load of pictures on the screen and had stopped at a picture of a very moody-looking silver-backed gorilla called Kabirizi. 'It says here that this guy is the "main male in a family of endangered mountain gorillas",' said Zed, reading the information. 'And, oh man! Listen to this! "An adult male gorilla can weigh as much as two hundred kilos!" Sheesh! I would *not* like to meet one of them on a dark night. Two *hundred*!'

'Is that a lot?' said Felix. He knew Dyson weighed about twenty-five kilos because the vet had weighed him the last time he'd been in for his vaccinations. 'How much do *you* weigh?' he asked his uncle.

Zed laughed. 'Under half of what this dude does – I'm around seventy kilos,' he said.

Felix's eyes bulged. A gorilla was twice the size of Zed! And Zed was already the tallest man Felix knew – his legs went on forever.

'OK, definitely not a gorilla then,' Felix said, shaking his head vigorously.

'An orang-utan?' Zed asked. 'Look at this hairy guy. Says here that "orang-utan" means "man of the forest".'

Felix read the information out loud: '"Orang-utans spend nearly all of their time in the trees. Every night they make nests, from branches and foliage in which they sleep. They are more solitary than other apes." What does "solitary" mean?' he asked.

'Means they're loners – they don't like company,' Zed explained.

Felix peered at the photo of the fluffy, scruffy, orange ape on the screen. 'That could be a good thing,' he said thoughtfully. After all, he wouldn't be able to have an orang-utan living inside the house with Dyson and Colin and Hammer anyway, not to mention with Mum and Dad and Merv. And if orang-utans liked sleeping in nests in the trees, there were two or three fantastic climbing trees out in the garden. Yes! The more Felix thought of it, the more he just knew that an orang-utan would be a much easier animal to look after than an elephant. Mind you, there was something about the expression on the orang-utan's face that reminded Felix a bit of Merv first thing in the morning. Felix frowned. He hoped the ape would not be as moody as his older brother.

'Hey, look at this one!' Zed hooted, pointing to a particularly fuzzy creature. 'He's called "Regis". What a great name! You could call him "Reggie".'

But Felix was not listening. He was already completely captivated by what he was reading on screen. Regis had been in a really bad way before the WWF had found him: he'd been raised by humans who had mistreated him and not given him enough food. How could anyone be so mean to such a clever, fun-loving animal? Felix had already made up his mind. He didn't care about the elephant idea any more. He didn't care what Flo said. He didn't even care if she went off with Millie Hampton and the Girly Pink Brigade and left him digging all the way to Australia on his own. He had decided: he was going to adopt an orang-utan. And not just any orang-utan. He was going to adopt Regis, bring him home and look after him forever.

9

FLO
GOES APE

Over tea, Mum and Silver and Zed got into a long and boring discussion about Energy. Felix didn't bother trying to follow the details of it. He knew that Zed thought people used too much of it and Mum thought Felix *had* too much of it. That's where he stopped trying to understand.

The one good thing about Boring Conversations was that they could be used as a cover for Much More Important Conversations. Felix leaned in close to Flo and told her about Regis.

'Flo,' he started in a low and determined tone, 'I need to talk to you urgently.'

'So do I!' said Flo, flicking a cautious look at the grown-ups. 'Silver says I might have been a monkey in a Previous Life. Apparently there is this thing called ree-in-kar-nay-shun, which I think is a different language and which means that you can have a life as an animal before or even after your life as a human, anyway—'

'Flo, it is animals that I need to talk to you about. Really, really urgently,' Felix hissed.

'Oh! Did you do it? Has Zed found you an elephant? What did he say about feeding it?' Flo asked. She was suddenly so excited that she did not seem to mind that Felix had interrupted her.

'That's exactly what I want to talk to you about,' Felix went on, his brain whirring as he tried to think of the most persuasive way of telling Flo that she was not going to get what she had thought she was getting, but something a whole lot better instead.

'Go on then!' Flo urged. She was shifting the bean part of her beany-cheese crunch from one side of the plate to the other to make it look as though she was eating it while dropping bits surreptitiously on

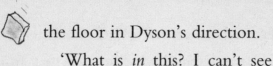

the floor in Dyson's direction.

'What is *in* this? I can't see anything that is truly real food for humans,' Flo muttered.

'It's OK once you get used to it. Put ketchup on it,' Felix advised, pushing the bottle towards her.

Flo shook her head violently and pulled an I-am-disgusted face. 'You were saying – about the elephant?'

'Actually it's an orang-utan,' Felix blurted out.

'What's an orang-utan?' Flora asked, frowning in puzzlement.

'The elephant – it's not an elephant any more, it's an orang-utan,' said Felix.

Flo gave a growl that sounded like an angry cat and pushed her plate away. 'Are you telling me that we are *not* getting an elephant?' she asked.

Felix crossed his arms grumpily and said rather loudly, forgetting that he didn't want Mum to be listening, 'I just think an elephant is a stupid idea – there is no way there is room for it in the house OR the garden! I have tried with cardboard boxes and it is what Dad would call a No Brainer. Whereas I have at least three trees which would fit an orang-utan and which are very fantastic for climbing, and that is what orang-utans like.'

Flo stared at Felix very hard. Felix shuffled his chair back from the table. He was worried that she might be able to melt him or zap him into tiny pieces with a stare like that. But he kept his resolve and said firmly: 'It's *my* birthday, and I don't want an elephant. I've decided. I want an orang-utan. He's been mistreated by nasty humans and he needs a good home. And he's called Reggie.'

'REGGIE?' Flo exploded. 'What kind of a stupid grandad-type

name is that? You are a weirdo, Felix Stowe.'

The grown-ups round the table had gone very quiet and were all watching this spectacle. Zed was the first to break the silence. 'Hey, guys – don't you like my cooking?' he asked.

Felix felt hot around the ears. 'No! I mean, yes, I do. Flo is just a Fussy Eater, that's all.'

Flo made a noise halfway between a gasp and a shout and crossed her arms grumpily. 'You are being horrible!' she cried. 'And I hate you and I hate beans *and* cheese *and* crunch and I absolutely TOTALLY hate orang-utans!'

'What's going on?' Mum asked sharply.

'Erm, Flo – ever had your hair braided?' Silver interrupted hastily.

'No. Why?' Flo asked with narrowed eyes.

'Well, I brought some stuff along to show you – wanna see?' Silver asked, pushing her chair back. 'Can we be excused, Marge?' she asked Mum.

'Good idea,' Mum said enthusiastically. 'Felix

can help me clear these plates and bring the pudding over.'

Zed winked at Felix. He waited until Flo and Silver had left the room and then whispered, 'Girls, eh? Will we ever understand them?'

Felix shook his head unhappily.

'Be cool, man,' said Zed. 'Whatever it is, nothing is a match for Silver's hair-braiding and chocolate brownies. Flo'll be a pushover after that, just you see.'

They went into the kitchen with the dirty plates and helped Mum stack the dishwasher and wash up the pots and pans and then they collected the strawberries and brownies to take back out to the table.

'If we're quick enough, we might be able to get a helping in while the girls are doing their hair,' Zed teased, reaching for the plate of brownies and snaffling a couple.

'Down, Dyson! Chocolate is really bad for dogs,' Felix cried, pushing Dyson's snout away from the plate.

'Down, Zed, as well for that matter!' Silver admonished. She had reappeared with a transformed Flo.

Felix nearly choked on the chunk of broken-off brownie Zed had shoved his way. Flo looked like a frightened hedgehog who had fallen into a magpie's nest and come out covered in bits of foil and multicoloured rubbish.

'Wha—?' Felix blurted out.

'Ah,' said Mum, biting her lip and trying not to laugh.

'Doesn't she look great?' Silver cut in quickly.

'Er,' said Felix.

'So. What's up?' Flo said casually, twirling a braid round her fingers and standing kind of sideways, with one hand on one hip: a position that she obviously thought made her look very grown-up and sophisticated. Like one of those people on the posters Merv had in his room. Not that Felix had ever had a proper close-up look at those posters, as Merv didn't let anyone go into his room. He had a handwritten notice on his door that said 'Come in here and you're dead', which sort of put Felix off.

Felix puffed noisily to cover up the panicky laughter fit that was building momentum in his chest.

Zed coughed loudly and said, 'Last one to the table gets NO chocolate!'

10
FELIX GOES
BANANAS

The next morning Flo told Felix that the minute she had got home her mum had made her take all the braids and bits of ribbon and beads out of her hair.

'And if it wasn't for the fact that having braids in your hair looks Totally Mega Lush, I am really not altogether positive that I will be going through that all over again in a hurry.'

Her mum had tugged and pulled so hard that Flo said she was sure her eyes were going to actually fall out of her head and roll on to the floor. 'It felt like my head was truly bleeding. I said to Mum, "You will have to take me to the Accident and Emergency place which is called A and E and they will make you sign a form to say that you have hurt your own child."'

But Mrs Small had not been worried about going to the A and E. She had been more worried about Flo 'looking like a rubbish tip' and had washed Flo's hair twice, which was not something Flo liked happening even once. The result of all the pulling and brushing and washing was that Flo's hair was extremely fly-away-ish the next day.

'Well, it serves you right, Flora Eleanor Small!' Her mum was still going on about it when they reached the pedestrian crossing right outside the school gates. 'I mean, I do not wish to be rude about your uncle's girlfriend, Felix, but doing Flora's hair like that on a school night? It is quite obvious that she does not have children of her own! And, Flora, you KNOW your teachers will not put up with—'

'Oh-KAY, Mum!' Flora interjected. 'Gotta go now – the bell's gone.'

Flo rolled her eyes at Felix as they leaped from the car, dragging their rucksacks behind them.

'Honestly, Mum is being quite impossible at the moment,' Flo huffed as she and Felix made it to the classroom with seconds to spare. 'And you should have heard her ranting when I just *mentioned* that it might be nice to have an orang-utan as a pet. I think to start with she thought my Extremely Brilliant Idea about the orang-utan was all a big joke. She laughed even more than a hyena when I told her that the reason for my Extremely Brilliant Idea was that Silver had said I had possibly been a monkey in a previous life, so it made sense that I would totally and utterly understand a monkey's brainwaves. And then Mum realized that I was absolutely deadly serious, so she just screamed at me about how it was a shame that I didn't put as

112

much effort into my General Good Behaviour as I did into coming up with crazy idiotic make-believe plans and that I was old enough now to really know better.'

'Wow,' said Felix. His eyes were out on stalks. He was sorely tempted to correct Flo over the minor detail that it had in fact been *his* Extremely Brilliant Idea to adopt an orang-utan instead of an elephant. But then he remembered Flo's mood from the night before.

'So,' he said tentatively, 'you reckon . . . an orang-utan?'

Flo arched one eyebrow at Felix and said, 'Absolutely. An orang-utan will make a perfect pet. After all you can play games with an orang-utan, Silver says. Silver says they are so intelligent. That would make sense about me being an ape in a previous life. Did you know they can actually work a computer? And Silver says that they make tools like humans do. Orang-utans make umbrellas for themselves out of big leaves when it rains, and they use sticks to get honey from beehives. They are very, very brainy. Silver says orang-utans have hands like humans! Not like – I don't know – *elephants*, for example, which do not even have hands and are so big and difficult to manage as pets. And they are used to being on their own because they are Solitary Beasts, so if we adopt one it will not be missing a huge family of other orang-utans, unlike an elephant, which lives in a group so it would miss all its relations. Honestly, who on earth would want something as huge as an *elephant* for a pet?' And she roared with laughter as if the whole idea was the most preposterous idea any living person could ever have.

'Right,' said Felix.

He couldn't help thinking that he had been let off very lightly. He had been expecting Flo to make him suffer an awful lot longer for changing their plans.

What a relief. He could stop worrying now and just get on with planning for the arrival of Reggie the orang-utan.

The next day, Felix didn't see that much of Flo as she had her music lesson at lunchtime, so she went into second lunch while Felix was out playing at the bug base on his own. Sometimes he was lonely when Flo wasn't there to do bug base with him, but sometimes he secretly quite liked it. Although she was his best friend, Felix thought that Mum was right when she said Flo could be a Bit Much. Besides, being on your own when you've got Things to Think About, like orang-utans and how to adopt them, was no bad thing.

At the end of the day Flo ran to catch up with

Felix as he made his way to the front to look out for Mum.

'So,' Flo said, pulling Felix round to face her and fixing him with a determined steely glare. 'What will it eat?'

'What will *what* eat?' said Felix.

'The orang-utan!' Flo said exasperatedly. 'I tried to ask you about it in that lesson on the Romans but you weren't listening.'

'Bananas, I s'pose?' offered Felix, yawning. It had been hard to concentrate on all those Invasions the Romans had done while at the same time worrying about how Mum would react when Reggie arrived. One of the only interesting facts about the Romans was that they had been used to having Really Wild Animals like lions around the place. It was a shame his mum was not a Roman, Felix pondered.

'Hmm,' Flo was looking thoughtful. 'But it can't

just be bananas. If you eat too many of them you get a Dire Ear, you know.'

Felix sat up. 'A Dire Ear? What is that?'

'It is something very bad which means you cannot go swimming or go to ballet lessons. It happened to Millie Hampton after Sophie Disbry's birthday party where they had all these banana-and-honey sandwiches, which Millie ate thirty-six of,' Flo said, with great authority.

Felix burst out laughing. 'Well, serves her right for being a great greedy whatsit! Anyway, we are not going to give the orang-utan banana-and-honey sandwiches, just bananas on their own. And I think that they eat other vegetables too.'

'A banana is not a vegetable,' said Flo.

'I never said it was,' Felix protested.

'You said that they eat "*other* vegetables"—'

'Flo!' Felix butted in. 'It doesn't matter, just listen – they eat vegetables and fruit – and probably peanuts as well. I can check in my book on apes anyway. So we'd better start collecting vegetables and fruit and peanuts for when the orang-utan comes to be adopted. By me,' he added firmly. Flo was not going to take over *that* part of the plan.

Flo stared hard into the distance for a moment and then she said, 'The vegetables are no problem at all. Dad is already starting to grow a load of disgusting things that I will never eat, so when they are grown I will pick them and give them to the orang-utan. What's his name? Ronnie?'

'Reggie. What kind of disgusting things?' Felix added suspiciously.

'Brussels sprouts,' said Flo, curling her top lip disdainfully.

'Uuuuurrrgh!' spat Felix. 'I'm *not* giving Reggie Brussels sprouts! They might poison him!'

Flo put her hands on her hips and said in a low,

menacing kind of voice, like those baddies on the telly who are mean but also a bit cool: 'The orang-utan will eat the Brussels sprouts, even if we have to wrap them in banana skins to fool it into thinking they are something more tasty than what they really are.'

Felix sighed heavily. He reminded himself that things could be a lot worse, so he swallowed all his words about Flo being a bossy old boot and instead he said, 'OK.'

Flo smiled. 'Great. So I'll be in charge of the Brussels sprouts then.'

Felix had a thought. 'When do the Brussels sprouts actually sprout?'

'What?'

'Well, what I mean is, normally you eat them for Christmas, and it's May now, so will they actually grow in time for Reggie to arrive? Cos, if I am getting Reggie for my birthday, that is only one week away.'

Flo put on her Mum-type voice and said, 'Don't worry about that. I'm sure it will be fine,' which didn't really answer Felix's question, but that was all she would say on the matter.

After Felix's mum had dropped Flo back at her house, Felix asked if he could go on the computer.

'Why?' Mum asked. 'Haven't you got some homework to do?'

Felix crossed his fingers behind his back and mumbled, 'I need the computer to do my homework, actually. It's all about orang-utans and their Habitat, which is a very scientific word which means "where animals live",' he added.

The phone started ringing, so Mum ran into the kitchen to answer it, calling over her shoulder, 'OK, but you'll have to get off it when Merv comes in cos he's got to finish his science project for tomorrow.'

Felix smiled. Using the word 'homework' had well and truly Put Mum Off the Scent.

He went into the study and turned on the computer. A fizzy feeling built up in his tummy as he thought of how perfect life with Reggie would be. Maybe Reggie would even teach him how to swing from the trees himself! Maybe once Mum had got used to the idea he might be allowed to spend one night a week up in the tree and he and Reggie could have sleepovers.

Felix spent the next half hour surfing the Internet for information about orang-utans. He found a very interesting site that told him exactly what he needed to know:

What do orang-utans eat?

Orang-utans eat mostly fruit – their favourites are huge spiky fruits called *Durian*. These fruits smell terrible, and taste a bit like custard and garlic, but orang-utans love them! Orang-utans also eat some flowers, honey, bark, leaves and insects.

How many babies do orang-utans have?

Orang-utans only have one baby at a time. There is a lot to learn about life in the forest and so babies stay with their mother and learn from her until they are seven or eight years old – this is longer than any other mammal except humans.

Where do orang-utans sleep?

Orang-utans sleep in nests in the trees which they make every day from leaves and branches. Orang-utans are arboreal, which means that they spend nearly all their time in the trees and hardly ever come to the ground. This makes them different from other apes like chimpanzees, gorillas and humans, who all spend a lot of time on the ground.

A fruit that tasted of custard and garlic? Felix wasn't sure he wanted to have anything to do with that. And would he have to go around collecting insects for Reggie to crunch on? No, Reggie would probably go out into the garden and find his own ants, Felix reasoned. And probably Mum would be pleased about that, because she hated it when there were ants' nests on the patio in the summer. She usually went out and put ant powder down to try and kill them.

Felix was about to shut down the site when Merv came into the study with his headphones on. He was wearing his worst kind of don't-come-near-me-or-I'll-flatten-you scowl, a beanie pulled down as far as it could go without blindfolding him and a pair of jeans showing so much underwear he might as well have gone without them altogether and worn just pants.

'Hey, low-life,' Merv snarled. 'Wot you up to? Let me guess . . .' He peered at the screen. 'Apes! I should have known. Figures anyway – takes one to know one. Har, har, har!'

Felix scuttled out of the room while his brother was too busy enjoying his own joke to thump him or throw something at him.

He ran into the kitchen. 'Mum! Did you buy any bananas or plums or any kind of fruit today?'

'Yes,' said Mum, looking puzzled. 'Why?'

'I'm – I'm *staaaaarving*!' said Felix, putting as much feeling into his voice as he could.

'Sorry? Am I hearing correctly? Or am I perhaps dreaming? My younger son who survives on a diet of Monster Pops, toast and chocolate is asking me for some FRUIT to EAT?' Mum said, talking to the wall in an over-the-top outraged and surprised kind of way.

'Yeah, well, I do love bananas you know that.'

'That's true,' Mum said, nodding. 'How could I forget the famous banana-tree incident?'

Felix blushed a bit. Then he crossed his fingers behind his back for the second time that day and ploughed on, 'And it's kind of part of my PSHE homework about, er, healthy eating,' he said. 'We have to eat some fruit, and then write down what it tasted like and, er, stuff like that,' he ended lamely.

'I thought you said your homework was to do with apes and their habitat?' Mum asked suspiciously.

'Oh, yes, that too,' Felix said. Rats, this was getting complicated. 'The PSHE homework is a week-long project where we have to write down all kinds of things about healthy food,' he said rashly. Uh-oh. This would mean healthy meals for a whole week now.

'OK,' said Mum. 'Take a look in the fruit bowl – we have some bananas and apples and a few oranges.'

'Great!' Felix rushed to the fruit bowl and helped himself to three bananas and two oranges.

'Hey!' Mum exclaimed. 'I'm cooking tea – don't ruin your appetite.'

Felix was already halfway up the stairs with the fruit in his hands. 'It's OK! I'm so hungry – I'll eat tea too.'

'And don't eat in your room! You'll only leave the skins lying around . . .'

The phone rang again, which meant Mum was distracted. Felix bolted up to his room and rummaged around under his bed until he found an old shoebox. It had once contained, amongst other things, a spider's nest, which Felix had been closely observing over the winter months. Unfortunately he had forgotten to observe it one week and in that time, the eggs had hatched and the spiders had ended up all over his room. Some had even got inside his pants and socks and stuff. It had been a bit tickly.

He put the bananas and the oranges in the box and stashed it back under his bed. I can add to this every day, he thought happily, and then by the time Reggie gets here there'll be loads of food for him to eat.

126

11
THE TRUTH ABOUT ADOPTION

Mum was unusually cheery when Felix came back downstairs. She was beaming all over her face and even occasionally chuckling to herself as if she'd just heard a fantastically funny joke on the radio. She often chuckled at the radio, although Felix could never understand what it was that she found so amusing. Most of the radio programmes she listened to were decidedly un-funny in his opinion.

It turned out it wasn't the radio, though, that had made her laugh.

'I have just had the most *hilarious* conversation with Flora's mum!'
she announced.

Felix felt all
the blood drain

from his face and an icy-cold hand grasped his insides. He did not like the sound of this 'hilarious conversation'. Mum and Mrs Small weren't even friends. They only ever rang each other to talk about the school run or whether or not it was a school trip or a spelling test that day.

Was Mum playing a trick on him? He shot her a very nervous glance. Or – much worse – had Flo Given the Game Away about Reggie?

He swallowed dryly before answering, 'Oh?'

'Yes! You wouldn't believe it, but Flora thinks you are getting an orang-utan for your birthday – as a *pet* to come and *live* with you *here*!' she guffawed.

Felix's icy innards did a double back-flip. What was Flo *thinking* of?

'Yes,' continued Mum cheerfully, 'apparently you were worried you didn't have enough food for it, so she's going to be getting all the Brussels sprouts from her dad's allotment that (and I'm quoting Flora here) "no one in their right mind ever wants to eat".'

Felix felt intensely sick. He had been betrayed! He realized now that he had not thought about the details of it, but he had assumed that Zed would bring Reggie round on his birthday and that Mum would not be able to do anything about it, because the orang-utan would come with all the information from the charity about how mistreated he had been and that would mean Mum couldn't be cruel and send him back.

But it was never going to work now. Mum was cross enough about Dyson and Colin and Hammer and the snails and the spiders and every other animal Felix had ever had anything to do with. She would never say yes to Reggie. Except, she was still smiling . . .

'Erm, but you're not cross?' Felix ventured.

Mum laughed again. 'Cross? How can I be cross? It's funny, that's all – and rather sweet.'

'Sweet?' Felix was puzzled. Was Mum starting

to talk like Uncle Zed? Did she mean 'sweet' as in 'it's cool that you are getting an orang-utan'? Or did she mean 'sweet' as in 'it's so cute'?

'Yes,' Mum went on, beaming. 'It's lovely that you and Flora play so imaginatively together. When I was your age I played "making house" or "cops and robbers" or things like that. But coming up with the idea of having an imaginary orang-utan – and opening your own zoo – it's amazing!'

Imaginary?

Then Felix thought again about what Flo's mum had said about 'make-believe plans' and everything fell into place. The mums thought this was all a game! Felix squirmed and shuffled on his chair and drew pictures with his finger on the wipe-clean tablecloth. How was he going to explain this? What would Mum say when she found out that Reggie really *was* coming to live with them? Would she make him cancel the adoption? And, if she did, what would happen to Reggie? Would he have to go back and live with the people who had raised him and made his life so horrible? Felix felt a wall of tears back up behind his eyes and a rush of words push against his throat and before he could stop to think things through properly, he had blurted: 'But it's *not* imaginary! The orang-utan really *is* coming to live with us. And he's called Reggie. Zed found him on the Internet.' And he went on to tell Mum all about Zed's promise to adopt him an animal for his birthday, and the research they had done on the WWF website.

As Felix spoke, he saw the smile on Mum's face fade away. Finally it had completely melted, leaving her with a distinctly stony expression.

'Ah,' she said. And then she said, 'Is that exactly, word for word, what that crazy brother of mine has told you?'

Felix gave a hard sniff to try and keep the tears at bay while he thought for a moment and then he said, 'Well, no. Not exactly word for word. But he has said that it would be cool to adopt me an orang-utan for my birthday. And when you adopt a child it comes to live in your house, doesn't it? So obviously that is what is going to happen with Reggie – he is going to come and live here. Otherwise what would be the point in doing the adoption thing?'

Mum grimaced. 'I think we need to get Zed over tonight to explain things,' was all she would say.

Unfortunately by the time Zed and Silver made it round, Mum had had a few more words to say on the topic of her 'crazy brother's ridiculous ideas'. The second Zed walked through the door, Felix launched himself into the hallway at his uncle, throwing his arms round his legs. Colin had been sitting in the middle of the floor, watching a spider, so he nearly got trampled on. He shrieked and streaked out of the front door, seconds before it closed, narrowly missing his tail.

'Mum says Reggie won't really come to live with us because that's not what animal adoption means, and I didn't believe her so she made me look it up on the Internet and read all the tiny, small words about what happens when you pay your money, and it says that Reggie will stay in Africa and it's just the charity that gets your money and all I get is the letters, but *you* said he was adopted and *I* thought—!'

Zed took a step back and held up both his hands in his 'cool it' gesture. 'Whoa, take a chill pill, man!' he

133

cried. 'You've gone, like, bright red.'

Dyson came in and jumped up on Zed, and set to enthusiastically licking him all over his face.

'I am NOT going to COOL IT!' Felix was yelling. He didn't care if he had gone multi-coloured rainbow: how could his uncle do this to him? He had never been this angry with Zed, ever. 'I thought you were the person who got it! No one else in my family ever understands how much I love animals. And you PROMISED I could have an animal for my birthday! YOU PROMISED!'

Zed brushed Dyson off him and shook his head in bewilderment, his mouth opening and closing just like Jonah the goldfish did that time Merv tipped him out of the tank to see what people meant by the expression 'a fish out of water'.

Silver put a hand on Zed's arm and gave him a look that said, 'I'll take things from here.'

'Felix,' she said gently. She crouched down until she was at the right height to talk to him face to face. 'Zed knows he's mucked up. And he's really sorry . . .'

Felix didn't care that Zed was sorry. He didn't care that Mum was looking at him from the doorway of the kitchen. He didn't care that Merv had just mooched his way downstairs to lean against the wall and enjoy the spectacle, smirking. Felix didn't care about anything.

'Zed?' Silver prompted.

Zed took Felix into his long gangly arms and squeezed him into a bear hug. 'Aw, don't cry, little dude,' he mumbled into Felix's hair. 'Silvs is so right. I'm totally sorry. I didn't realize you thought this adoption was, like, for real.'

Silver said, 'What say we go out for pizza and we talk about it, hey?'

Zed held Felix away from him and chucked him under his chin, using a thumb to wipe away a couple of stray tears. 'Silvs always knows how to make things right — what do you say, man?'

Felix looked up at his uncle. He felt watery and weak from all his shouting and crying. He knew deep down that Zed had not meant things to turn out this way. And he still had enough faith in his uncle to hope that he had a solution to the situation. Felix managed a smudged smile and nodded.

'Marge! We're off out to Veggie Heaven for pizza. I'll sort this, no worries!' Zed yelled in the direction of the kitchen.

Silver winked at Felix and grinned.

At least that was one good thing that had come out of the evening, thought Felix. He wouldn't have to eat the stew Mum was cooking, which was beginning to smell a bit like Dyson's food would if you tried to heat it up.

'Wow, Veggie Heaven, what a blast – for *nerds*,' sneered Merv, slouching his way back up to his room and slamming the door. Seconds later music was pounding through the floorboards and making the pictures on the wall shake in their frames.

'MERVIN!' Mum wailed.

'Come on,' said Zed, throwing Felix a friendly punch on the shoulder. 'Let's split while the going's good.'

12
PLANS CHANGE

The thing about being with Zed and Silver was that the minute you were around them life immediately looked and felt a whole lot warmer and glowier. Even going to Veggie Heaven was fun, and Felix wasn't exactly what you would call Keen On Vegetables. But Veggie Heaven wasn't all nut roasts and bean burgers and tofu Bolognese. They did the most amazing pizzas on the planet with such a rich gloopy tomatoey sauce (with No Bits) and so much stringy chewy cheese and such a mountain of tangy black olives (which are too delicious to count as vegetables), that really it didn't feel like you were eating anything remotely healthy. Felix was soon stuffing his mouth full of steaming pizza, sauce dripping down his chin, and his brain in complete and utter Neutral. Silver prodded Zed, and Zed shuffled awkwardly.

'The thing is, right, there's adoption and then there's adoption,' Zed began, rather vaguely.

'Good start,' muttered Silver.

Zed shot her a helpless look and strummed his long fingers on the table as if he would be able to extract some words from the shiny metal surface. 'OK,' he started again. 'Like, there's adopting a kid cos you really want one of your own but you can't . . . and then of course you get to take the kid home with you, else what'd be the point? And then there's adopting, like, a kitten or a puppy from the RSPCA cos someone's abandoned it? And then you get to take that home too, cos puppies and kittens are normal pets that loads of people have in their houses. And then there's these adoption *schemes* like the ones we were looking at on the Net where you pay money every month to a charity who looks after animals, often in other countries, and the animal gets to stay in its *own* home and be looked after properly with all the money that you are kindly sending it.'

Felix was struggling with an extra-long stringy piece of cheese and frowning as he tried to fit it into his mouth. His fingers were covered in tomato sauce by now, and the front of his hoody wasn't much better off.

Zed interpreted the confused expression on Felix's face to mean that he had not explained the whole adoption thing clearly enough. As it turned out, he had. But Felix was enjoying the pizza so much that he had not been listening very carefully.

Silver bit her lip. 'Do you get what Zed is saying, Feels?'

Felix wiped his mouth with the back of his hand and said, 'What?'

Zed sighed and put his head in his hands. He rubbed his head for a moment and then looked up and said wearily, 'We didn't know you thought Reggie was coming to *live* with you. Thing is, he'd hate it here. It's too cold and he'd miss his natural habitat. At least you know with the adoption money that we've sent that he'll be well looked after. You'll see that from the emails and photos the charity sends every month.'

Felix pulled an I-suppose-so face. 'But what about monkeys in zoos?' he asked suddenly. 'Or in those safari park places, like Shortfleet where we're going for my birthday treat? They have monkeys there. Isn't it too cold there? Why don't those monkeys get sent back to Africa or Asia where they are supposed to live?'

Zed nodded seriously. 'You're right there,

man. But it's complicated, y'know: some of those monkeys were born right here in the UK, so they don't know any different.'

'Are you saying that the animals at Shortfleet are Born In Captivation?' Felix asked, outrage filling every word.

Zed winced and said, 'Yeah. But, man, it's not a bad thing,' he added hastily. 'For instance, wouldn't you prefer for the animals to be born in captivity in this country where people can look after them well and feed them good food and protect them rather than have them be born in another country where they might be shot or maltreated like Reggie has been? Lord Basin set up Shortfleet for that very reason. It's like I told you: he's a well-respected dude in the conservation world.'

Felix puffed out his cheeks in disgust. A splodge of pizza escaped from the corner of his mouth. 'First you say that it's better that when you adopt an animal it stays in its own country because it

142

would be too cold here, and now you are telling me that being Born In Captivation is better because the animal will not be maltreated! You are not making an actual word of sense,' he complained.

Zed's face was a picture of confusion and panic. 'Er . . .' he said.

'Hey, I know,' Silver chirruped. 'Let's have the toffee-fudge ice cream, yeah?'

Felix pursed his lips and thought for a moment. 'OK,' he said. It was quite clear that Zed had no idea what he was talking about, so there was not much point in continuing the conversation. 'Can I have chocolate sprinkles?' he asked.

'Sure you can,' said Silver.

Zed made a big show of calling over the waitress and ordering just about every kind of ice cream accessory he could think of:

'Chocolate sprinkles, right? And do you have those awesome little paper umbrella dudes to stick in the top?

And maybe like a sparkler too? And marshmallows – we *have* to have marshmallows – it's like compulsory . . .'

And while he was doing that Felix chewed over the conversation he had just had with his uncle and Silver. So, he thought, this is what has happened so far: Number One, I cannot have an elephant as a pet as it is too big and Mum would Never Allow It. Number Two, I cannot adopt an orang-utan as it is too cold in this country and the charity people would Never Allow It. Number Three: it is, however, possible to let wild animals live in this country if they are Born In Captivation by a Responsible Breeder like Lord Basin. He knew there was the beginning of a solution to his pet problem here, but he couldn't quite see how it all fitted together just yet.

'Da-daaaaah!' Zed said with an enthusiastic flourish of a long gangly arm.

Felix blinked at the ginormous knickerbocker glory that had just been put in front of him.

'One mammoth ice cream with everything I could think of on top!' Zed announced goofily. 'For my favourite nephew – to say sorry,' he added quietly. 'Are we cool now, man? I'll still pay for the adoption and you'll get the newsletters and info pack and stuff . . .'

'Maybe we can look into another treat for you when we visit Shortfleet?' Silver said, as Felix tucked into his dessert. 'You know, like sometimes they let people be keeper for the day where you get to help out with the animals. They have so many animals in that place, I'm sure they could do with someone to take them off their hands once in a while,' she added.

'Thanks,' said Felix, feeling a little brighter suddenly. He took hold of the long-handled spoon that had come with his ice cream and dug it deep into the dessert mountain in front of him.

145

Silver's words echoed glitteringly in his mind as he shovelled a large portion of ice cream and chocolate sprinkles into his mouth. 'You know, Silver, you have actually given me a mega-fantastic idea.'

Silver frowned and started to say something, but Zed shook his head at her and said cheerily, 'Here's to the coolest birthday ever, dude!'

'It's all over,' Felix announced dramatically to Flo the next day in the playground. They had not gone to school together that morning as Mrs Small had called to say Flo was 'being difficult' and so they were 'running late'.

'What is all over?' Flo asked stroppily. 'The world? The game you were playing with Harris over there when you wouldn't let me in? The snack you were eating, which you wouldn't—'

'If you will just stop talking for one tiny micro-nanosecond and actually listen for a change, I will tell you,' Felix interrupted crossly. Then he took a deep breath and plunged in quickly: 'I am not getting a real live orang-utan for my birthday after all.' And he proceeded to tell Flo what had happened the night before.

To her credit, Flo did at least wait until Felix had finished before sinking her head into her hands and wailing: 'Oh no!' Her bouncy curls flopped over the top of her head and made her look like a floor mop of blonde fluff.

Felix grimaced. She wasn't going to start crying, was she? He didn't like it when girls cried. Should he pat her on the back? Should he go and get a teacher or one of Flo's girly friends? But then the curls were tossed back into place and Flo looked up at him with a steely flash of anger in her eye.

'Just answer me one question, Felix Stowe,' she said venomously.

'Oh-Kay . . .' Felix faltered.

'What am I supposed to do now with all those bananas? And all those EXTRA Brussels sprouts

147

Dad has planted – how am I going to get out of eating them? Because Dad really believes I'm going to, you know. I lied to him, all for YOUR sake, and told him that I had decided I loved them! This is a total disaster. Are YOU going to come to my house and eat Brussels sprouts for tea for months? I think you should, actually. As a punishment for getting me into this in the first place,' she finished.

Felix was going to respond by saying, 'That is not really just one question.' He also thought of pointing out how interesting it was that, now that everything had gone so disastrously wrong, Flo was back to saying that adopting Reggie had been *his* idea. But he thought better of saying both those things, especially as Flo had folded her arms across her chest in her most fearsome pose and was glaring at him.

Felix trembled a bit, but he told himself he wasn't going to let Flo intimidate him this time. He had already thought up a plan to solve his lack-of-exotic-pet-ness that was so unbelievably marvellous and daring that even Flo Small would not be able to think of a single contradictory thing to say about it. A smile slowly spread across his face as he prepared to announce it.

'Well, I'm glad you think the idea of eating twelve million tonnes of Brussels sprouts is so utterly hilarious,' Flo barked.

But Felix's plan was so brilliant that he found himself laughing in Flo's face. 'I will not have to eat all those sprouts,' he announced defiantly. 'And nor will you,' he put in hastily before Flo could start on him again. 'Just listen to my plan.'

And as Flo listened her eyes grew wider and wider and her cheeks grew pinker and pinker, until finally she said, 'Felix Stowe, you are a genius!'

GENIUS!

13
BİRTHDAY
BOY

The next few days dragged so Impossibly Slowly that Felix was convinced someone had got hold of time and shaken it around and then dropped it on the floor so that it had stopped working properly. In fact, there were occasions where he could have sworn that it had actually started going backwards. But at last, by some huge miracle, time made up its mind to start working again and the morning of the birthday arrived.

Felix awoke with Colin sitting on his head.

'Hey, get off, you overgrown fur hat!' he mumbled, swatting at his cat as he sat up in bed.

Colin stretched, his claws twanging out one by one in a rather dangerous fashion. Then he gave

Felix one of his looks.

Felix ignored him and glanced around his room, trying to work out why he had woken up with a bubbly, fizzy feeling inside him. It was the kind of feeling he got when he was really excited about something, but today he couldn't for the life of him remember what it was he had to feel excited about.

He looked at the poster of the kingfisher, which was one of his favourites, as it was a close-up of the bird with a silvery fish in its beak. He had always wanted to get that close to a kingfisher in real life.

Then he found himself looking at his ultimate, best and most favouritest poster of all: the one of the orang-utan hanging from a branch with one hairy arm, its feet clamped together like two human hands clapping. And then he remembered what he had to feel so excited and fizzy and bubbly and poppy about.

'Yippeeeeeeeeee!' he yelled, leaping from his duvet and sending Colin shooting under the bed.

'It's my BIRTHDAY!' And he did a Victorious Dance of Glory around the room, hopping from one foot to the other and making monkey noises in between singing various versions of 'Happy Birthday' including the one about going to the zoo and seeing a fat monkey. As he danced and sang, he pulled off his pyjama bottoms and threw them around the room, adding to the scene of general Mayhem and Devastation that already surrounded him.

Mum poked her head round the door at one point and mumbled something about it being five o'clock and could he please 'put a sock in it'. But Felix would not have known where to find a sock in the war zone that was his room, even if he had wanted to, so he just ignored Mum and carried on dancing and whooping and oo-oo-ooing until eventually Dad came in and shouted: 'Felix, it is FIVE THIRTY and if you think I'm going to drive you to Shortfleet for the day on limited sleep, you've got another think coming, young man, birthday or no birthday. So GO BACK TO BED!'

Felix did stop the rumpus then. The last thing he wanted was for his trip to Shortfleet to be cancelled, especially when his Marvellous Plan depended on going there.

I should get ready, he thought, looking at his alarm clock. I've only got three hours.

He pushed all his wildlife magazines into a sort of tidy-ish pile under his bed, then he found some clothes that kind of matched from various places around the room and got dressed standing on the free patch of floor. Then he fished around under his bed again and pulled out a secret box of stuff that he had been saving. Colin was still under there, sulking.

Then Felix sat down on the edge of the bed and ran through the plan in his head.

He looked at the alarm clock again.

'Only a quarter to six!' he groaned. 'No one will be up for AGES yet.' He sighed. It was always like this on his birthday. He was not allowed to wake up Mum and Dad until seven o'clock to open his presents, but *he* woke up at least two hours before this.

I've planned my plan and I've got my Secret Stuff, so what else can I do while I wait? he thought to himself. His stomach rumbled noisily. It gave him an idea. 'Aha!' he said aloud. 'I'll make a big surprise breakfast for everyone. That will cheer them up and stop them moaning at me.'

He raced downstairs so fast he skidded over the last four stairs as if he was tobogganing and flew over Dyson who had been snoozing on the bottom step.

Dyson trotted into the kitchen after Felix, who

fed him, let him out, put some food out for Colin (who was *still* hiding under Felix's bed) and went to put some hamster food in Hammer's cage. Then he set to work laying the table for everyone, and when he had finished he sat down and waited.

'You've laid the table for breakfast!' Mum exclaimed when she emerged later, looking bleary-eyed and a bit smudged. Her face was never quite her own face until she'd had a cup of coffee. Or two. She blinked and shook her head in a way that suggested that she did not believe what she was seeing. 'Wonders will never cease.'

Felix was particularly proud of the way he had laid the table. He had put fruit in the fruit bowl and put that in the middle of everything as a kind of decoration.

Then he had made sure that all the plates and bowls and mugs were matching for once, even though this had meant he had had to unstack the dishwasher and put all the other bits and bobs of washing-up on the work surfaces as he was not sure which cupboards to put them away in. (It made the kitchen look a little like the china department in one of those big posh shops in town, but at least he hadn't broken anything.)

And then he had put four bowls out, and just for a change and because it looked pretty, he had put the plates on top of the bowls. It had the rather pleasing effect of making the place settings look like mushrooms. To finish it all off, he had balanced a mug on each plate and put a knife and a spoon in each mug.

'I should get a job in a restaurant to earn some money,' he had said aloud when he stepped back to admire his handiwork. 'Then I could buy all the animals in the world that I have ever wanted.'

Mum sat down and gingerly removed her mug from her plate, and took the plate carefully off the bowl and filled it with her favourite cereal, known by Dad as 'Sawdust Muck', but labelled on the packet as 'Healthy Hearty Muesli'.

'Would you like some coffee, Mum?' Felix asked in his politest voice.

'Am I still asleep?' Mum asked, blinking again. 'I didn't know you knew how to make coffee. I hope you were careful with the kettle.'

'Oh, I didn't use the kettle,' said Felix cheerily.

'Er, what *did* you use?' Mum asked. She was suddenly looking distinctly less eager at the prospect of a reviving hot drink.

'The hot tap!' said Felix, feeling very pleased with himself. This really had been a fantastic idea of his, making breakfast. Mum would be so happy about it that it would put her in a good mood for the rest of the day, and she would not mind a bit when it came to his plan . . .

'Ah,' said Mum. 'Erm, it's OK. I'll just have orange juice, thanks.'

Felix shrugged. 'All right. I'll leave this for Dad then.' He put the coffee pot on the kitchen table and sat down to tuck into his own breakfast.

Mum breathed out heavily, then shooting Felix an anxious glance she said cautiously, 'It was lovely of you to get everything ready.' She made a stab at her Sawdust Muck and peered at it as if she was worried something might be living in it. Like a hamster, for example. It did look like the shavings in Hammer's cage.

'You're not, er, trying to tell us something, are you?' Mum continued, grimacing slightly.

'Noooo!' Felix protested, munching on a slice of toast. 'I only wanted ev'ryone to have a nice bre'kf'st.'

Mum smiled, but it looked painful. 'That's lovely.'

'Is Merv coming to Shortfleet?' Felix asked

anxiously, glancing over his shoulder at the kitchen door. It would be just like Merv to do something stupid and ruin Felix's plan.

Dad had come in and poured himself a huge mug of coffee. 'Merv? Get up on a Saturday morning? Merv come on a family outing?' He took a large gulp of coffee and immediately his face went tight as if he'd just sucked a lemon, and he spluttered the coffee down his chin. 'Who made this? It's revol—'

'What your dad's trying to say is, "No, Merv's not coming,"' said Mum hastily, frowning at Dad and shaking her head.

'Thank goodness for that,' Felix said with feeling. 'And what time are Flo and Zed getting here?'

'Not till eight,' said Dad, wiping his mouth on the back of his pyjama sleeve and glancing at his watch in a woebegone way. 'D'you know, sometimes I think Merv's got the right idea. It's still only half past seven . . .'

Only half past seven! Felix sighed. They weren't due to leave for the safari park until half past eight. How could any normal human being be expected to wait another Whole Hour before setting off on the birthday treat of the century? Not to mention the agony of waiting until he could put his amazing plan into action.

Felix felt a howl work its way up from his belly, and just about stopped himself from letting it out. Instead a tiny groan emerged from his lips.

Mum smiled. 'Why don't you open a few presents while you're waiting, and then you can help me pack some snacks for the day?' she asked. 'I've bought crisps and chocolate and things, and we can make sandwiches.'

Felix perked up immediately. He had been so overexcited about the day itself and the plan that he had almost forgotten about presents and party food.

Then he remembered something else. 'You did

buy those peanuts I asked you to get, didn't you?'
he quizzed his mum. 'And we must take loads of
bananas – Flo *loves* bananas almost as much as I do,'
he added quickly, noticing the suspicious looks
Mum was giving him.

'Felix,' said Dad, 'you've been eating nothing
but bananas these days as far as I can see. You'll
turn into one if you're not careful. Ho! Ho!'

Felix curled his lip. Dad's jokes were rarely
funny, but that had to be the worst one in a while.

Mum rolled her eyes and said, 'I did get the
peanuts, yes, but I'm still not entirely sure why we
had to have so many packets. There's only five of
us going on this outing, and Dad doesn't even like
peanuts. Come to think of it, isn't Clive allergic to
them?'

'No, no,' said Felix
firmly. 'Uncle Zed loves
them. He actually asked
me to make extra-specially sure that we would

definitely have bags and bags of them, cos he's got a Bit of a Craving going on for peanuts just now.'

'Hmm,' said Mum, not looking altogether convinced with this explanation. 'As for the bananas, I didn't think Madam ate any fruit.'

'Madam' was Mum's name for Flo – not when Flo was around, of course; that would have been rude.

'Flo *does* like bananas,' Felix assured her. 'She actually positively ADORES them. She would eat them all the time if her mum was as kind as you are and actually let her.'

Mum narrowed her eyes at the totally unexpected and quite unusual compliment her younger son had just paid her. Then she sighed and started clearing away the breakfast things. 'OK,' she said. 'Well, when you've opened the presents in the sitting room, you can go and look for some Tupperware boxes and I'll get the snacks out, bananas, peanuts and everything. You can help me pack the picnic.'

Felix went into the sitting room where there were three presents waiting for him. He sat down slowly and made himself focus on the shiny wrapping paper and the bows and ribbons. He was nine now and it was really important to be Mature about this. He knew that he should not do what he normally did. But his fingers were wriggling, a big bubble was working its way up inside him . . .

'Aieee!' he cried, throwing himself at the presents like a dog leaping on to a big fat juicy bone. He ripped the paper off all three presents in the space of five seconds, scooped up the contents and went tearing down the hall shouting, 'I've got a bat box and a wormery and a real live woodlouse house! Cool!' He had been wanting a wormery since forever so that he could make his own compost, and the bat box would be wicked for hanging in the trees and

watching bats zoom in and out on
a summer's evening and as for the
woodlouse house – who wouldn't want one
of those?

'You like the presents then?' Dad said, ruffling
his son's hair as he whizzed past.

'I LOVE THEM!' Felix yelled. This was surely
going to be the best birthday ever.

He threw himself into the sandwich-
making with gusto, smearing mayonnaise
on top of slices of ham, slapping the
ham between slices of bread and poking
gherkins and bits of that plasticky cheese
with the holes into everything in sight. Mum
complained the kitchen looked like a bomb had hit
it, but Felix thought this was a slight exaggeration,
as bombs would make craters in everything and
would most likely reduce the walls of the house to
rubble too. But he was very determined to be good
and helpful, so he grabbed a cloth and scrubbed

at the table to show willing. Then he scrambled upstairs to do a last-minute check on his own bit of organization for the day.

He shut his bedroom door and tiptoed over to where he had stashed his rucksack. Mum had given him the peanuts as he had insisted that he wanted to be helpful and carry them, but she had Drawn the Line at giving him the bananas. 'They will go all squishy,' she had told him. 'Especially if you've stuffed your bag full of all the normal nonsense you insist on taking with you on car journeys.' She was probably right, Felix thought. He would just have to make sure that Zed was allowed to look after the bananas so that he had Easy Access to them in the back of the car.

Felix carefully shut the bag and slung it over one shoulder. Then taking a last look around his room he smiled to himself. His plan was going to work like clockwork.

14
WE'RE GOING TO
THE ZOO, ZOO, ZOO!

DRIIIING!

'At last!' Felix yelled, zooming downstairs on his bottom to get to the door as fast as possible.

'Hey!' Zed cried, flinging his arms in the air. He was holding an interesting-looking parcel in one hand, Felix noticed. 'Happy birthday, man!' Zed started singing, 'We're going to the zoo, zoo, zoo, and you can come too, too, too . . . Ooo, ooo, ooo!' He finished with a pretty cheesy impression of a monkey, jumping about, his long arms dangling by his sides.

Felix flinched at the sight. Why had Zed chosen to impersonate a monkey? Surely he didn't suspect anything . . . ?

But when Zed stopped abruptly and looked a bit sheepish, Felix realized it was just his uncle up to his usual silly jokes.

'We are *not* going to the zoo! Shortfleet is a safari park,' Felix said importantly, before hurling himself at Zed in an affectionate rugby tackle.

Zed chuckled. 'I know, sorry. Hey! I've got something for you. Cool it a minute, man. You might break the present,' he gasped, as Felix's rough-and-tumble tickling attack got a bit over-boisterous. He gently pushed Felix back and handed him the interesting-looking parcel, which was wrapped in brown paper and held together with a sliver of gold ribbon.

'But you've already given me a present,' Felix reminded him. 'The orang-utan, Reggie – remember?'

Zed blushed. 'Yeah, but me and Silvs, we just felt bad about that, dude. Y'know – all that stuff about you thinking he really was coming to live with you. We thought we should give you something for real. Sorry Silvs couldn't come too, by the way. No room in your dad's car for the both of us. She wanted to give you this, as well,' Zed added, picking up a plastic bag he'd placed by the door. 'But you'd better open the other present first.'

'Thanks!' said Felix as he walked towards the kitchen. 'Flo's not here yet. Do you want a drink?' he called over his shoulder.

Mum came out to say hello. 'I wouldn't recommend the coffee,' she said, raising one eyebrow.

'Why not?' Felix protested, but he didn't really care. He was in too much of a hurry to open the present.

Zed grinned. 'It's OK. I'm not into coffee any more, sis,' he said. 'Gives me the shakes, y'know?'

Mum smiled wryly. 'Oh?' she said. 'OK, well have some mint tea if you like. I'll put the kettle on.'

'OH WOW!' Felix yelled, holding up the object he'd just freed from the brown paper. 'Look at this, Mum! It's soooooo wicked!'

Mum frowned. 'What is it?' she asked.

'It's a butterfly and moth kit! I've ALWAYS wanted one!' he cried, dancing round and round in a circle and whooping madly. 'You put the caterpillars in the caterpillar home with loads of sugary stuff and then you watch them change into butterflies or moths. Woooo!'

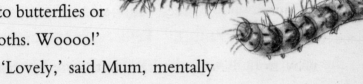

'Lovely,' said Mum, mentally

clocking up how many mini-beast houses and other animal homes she was going to have to dust around from now on.

Dyson rushed in from the garden and was soon adding to the commotion by barking and leaping all over the place.

'DYSON, OUT!' Mum yelled, pointing to the

back door. 'OOOOH, there's mud everywhere, and just when we were ready to go.'

'Can I see what's in the bag now?' Felix asked.

Zed nodded and handed it over, carefully taking the caterpillar kit back so that Felix had a free pair of hands.

The contents of the bag resulted in even more jumping and leaping and shouting: 'A BIRD'S NEST!' Felix shrieked. 'FOR MY COLLECTION!'

'Yeah, it's an abandoned blackbird's nest, man. Make sure you label it.'

'WHOOOPPPEEEE!' Felix yelled, punching the air in delight with the hand that wasn't holding the nest.

'Can't you lot shut up?' Merv emerged, low-slung pyjamas revealing more than anyone would ever want to see, his hair sticking up in so many different positions that he looked more like a porcupine than any real live one.

'Merv!' Mum admonished. 'You could at least

say happy birthday to your brother.'

'"Happy birthday to your brother",' Merv sneered, and then for good measure he added: 'Squirt!' and disappeared back up to his bedroom, slamming the door behind him.

Felix put the nest down on the kitchen table before throwing his arms round Zed and squeezing him. 'You are the best uncle in the whole wide world.'

Zed laughed.

DRIIIING!

'Yay!' Felix shouted, hurling himself at the front door. 'That'll be Flo – time to GO!'

Felix ran to the front door and flung it open so hard he almost caught Zed in the face.

'Wow, chill a bit, man,' said Zed. 'Have you been at your mum's coffee or something?'

'Hi, Flo!' Felix almost screamed he was so toppled-over with excitement.

Flo did actually scream. 'Aaaaiiiieeee!' She

171

jumped up and down and up and down, sending her mad hair into an even madder frenzy of frizziness.

Mrs Small stood at the end of the drive and waved cautiously. 'See you later, darling. Have a lovely birthday, Felix!' she called. 'Good luck . . .' she added, raising her eyebrows rather pointedly at Zed.

Flo waved vaguely in the direction of her mother and then continued shrieking and bouncing up and down.

'OK, OK. That's enough,' said Mum, coming out of the kitchen wearing a pair of rubber gloves and carrying a bottle of cleaning liquid in her hands. 'This has been a very long morning as it is, what with Felix 'Dawn Chorus' Stowe here giving the house a make-over with mayonnaise and ham and then Dyson charging in and redecorating it all over again with mud.'

'What?' said Flo, stopping in mid-scream to stand and gawp at Mum.

'Never mind,' said Mum. 'Are you ready to go?'

Flo's excitement withered under the force of Mum's glower and she stopped jumping. 'I'm sorry,' she said breathlessly, 'but this is just about the best day of my whole life and that's pretty amazing as it's not even *my* birthday, it's Felix's, but it's still the best day ever because we are finally going to get our hands on some real mon—'

'BLEURGHOOOOW!' Felix let out an almighty spluttering cough while crunching his eyebrows together very fiercely indeed in Flo's direction.

'Felix! Put your hand up, please,' Mum admonished. 'Flora does not want to be covered in germs and breakfast and goodness knows what else.'

'Yes, Felix,' said Flo. 'You are being utterly gross. And why are you growling and frowning like that?'

Felix rolled his eyes and mouthed, 'Shut up about the you-know-what!'

'Oh, OK,' she said carelessly. 'Anyway, happy birthday!' Her voice rose to a squeak at the end of the sentence and she started jumping again while she thrust a parcel into Felix's hands. 'I couldn't wait to give you this.'

Felix grinned. 'Thanks, Flo.' He started ripping the paper off and revealed a slim plastic box with cartoon images of animals all over the front. Felix stared at it, completely speechless, his jaw hanging open.

'Don't you – you do like it, d-don't you?' Flo stammered, waiting like an anxious puppy for Felix's reaction.

'Like it? Are you kidding?' he finally whispered.

And then: 'I LOVE IT!' he shouted, flinging himself at Flo as if he was about to hug her and then changing his mind in mid-fling and messing up her crazy fluffy hair instead.

Flo was grinning so hard that every tooth, and every gap between every tooth, was on show. She was in danger of starting another performance of the high-pitched variety, when Zed gently prised Felix's hands from her hair and said, 'Are you going to tell me what it is?'

Felix looked at him as if he had just said something in Japanese. 'How can you not know what this is?' he asked in total disbelief, waving the box in front of his uncle's face. 'It's Zoo Mania!'

Zed smiled and shook his head. 'Whatever you say, dude.'

Flo shook her head and sighed impatiently. 'Honestly, don't you even know what Zoo Mania is? What kind of an Olden-Fashioned-Day person are you? It's a computer game, of course. You get to build up your own zoo with animals and feed them and look after them and be a real zookeeper, except not really in real true life, obviously. Not *yet* anyway,' she added cryptically, shooting Felix a knowing look.

Zed caught her at it and said, 'Yet?'

Felix's face twisted itself into a mask of horror, but luckily Mum re-emerged at that very moment. (She was looking rather weary considering the day had only just got going, Felix thought.)

'OK, no more time to stand and natter,' she said. 'Dad's getting the car out and the lunch is packed and we're all here. So let's go!'

15

MONKEYING
AROUND

The driveway to Shortfleet safari park was the longest driveway in the world, according to Flo.

'You've been down a lot of driveways in your time then?' Dad asked, chuckling.

'Oh millions,' said Flo airily. 'And this is definitely the most longest of the lot. Which is rather annoying,' she added grimly, 'as it means it's going to take us even more time to actually arrive in the safari park.'

Felix agreed. 'It has been *such* a long journey. Are we nearly there yet?'

'ARRRGHHH!' chorused Mum and Dad.

'Hey, chill,' said Zed. 'Time is all in the mind, y'know—'

'*Clive*,' Mum warned.

Zed bit his lip and made a zipping motion with his hand while giving Flo and Felix a mammoth-sized wink.

'I wonder if, like, the dude himself will be in residence today,' Zed said, gazing out of the window at the huge house at the bottom of the Longest Drive in the World.

'The who?' asked Flo.

'Lord Basin,' said Felix knowledgeably. 'He is a Very Important Person in the World of Conversationism. Isn't he, Zed?'

'I think Flora would win the prize for "conVERsationism",' giggled Mum.

'It's "conSERvationism",' Zed explained as Felix and Flo looked at him with a puzzled expression. 'And you're bang on the button, man. Lord Basin is cool on conservation and he is way far out too.'

'Far out where?' said Flo.

Zed laughed. '"Far out", as in he's a wacky kinda guy! He dresses in these awesome long cloaks and he always wears a funky hat. And I've heard stories about his house like you wouldn't believe, man. They say he has carpets that move and buttons in the wall that you can push to open secret passageways. And there are all the artefacts and sculptures that he's brought back from his travels in Africa.' Zed had a dreamy look on his face now. He often got that look on his face when he started thinking of Africa. Felix sometimes worried that his uncle would end up going back there and then he wouldn't be able to see him so much.

At last, after far too many verses of 'She'll Be Coming Round the Mountain' (which included a distinctly unusual 'She'll be wearing big bananas when she comes . . .' from Felix who could hardly breathe for laughter by the time it was over) the Stowes, Zed and Flo arrived at the entrance.

'Welcome to Shortfleet Safari Park,' read a placard. 'Please read the safety notices and stay in your vehicle at all times.'

'Oh no!' Flo cried. 'Why do we have to stay *in* the vee-high-kel?'

Felix jabbed her firmly in the ribs. 'It's pronounced *veer-kul*, you loony,' he cried, and then in a low voice 'and shut up about getting out or anything like that or you'll Give the Game Away!'

'But—' Flo protested, rubbing her ribs.

'Remember what I said about the plan,' Felix hissed. 'We don't need to get out.'

'Why?' Flo persisted.

Felix started whispering and gesturing wildly at the car windows.

'Oh, right,' said Flo, sitting back and smiling smugly.

'What are you two up to?' Mum
demanded, swivelling round in her seat
to eyeball the squirming pair. 'Can't you squash
them or something, Clive?'

'They're cool, sis,' Zed said, putting an arm
round each child. 'They're just excited, that's all.'

'No thanks to your crazy stories and all that
stupid singing,' Mum muttered.

'Hey, look – a giraffe!' Zed shouted.

Dad had pressed the button to open his window
and was paying the entrance fee. Felix strained to
look out of the windscreen at the enclosure beyond
the car park. His eyes bulged. Giraffes were grazing
on nets full of leaves that had been strung up in the
trees for them.

'Wow, it's weird to see giraffes in a field like that!'
he said. And it just proves that wild endangered

animals *can* live in England, he thought.

'Sit back down, Felix,' said Mum. 'You've got to stay strapped in.'

Dad thanked the keeper and put the window back up. 'We've got a CD to listen to as we go round,' he said, handing a square envelope to Mum. 'It's read by that Kitty Bumble off the telly – you know the one that does the bird-watching programme with that old man with the beard?'

'The ditzy, giggly, blonde one?' Mum teased, taking the CD out of its packaging and posting it into the car CD player.

Felix thought the back of Dad's ears had gone a bit hot-looking. 'Kitty Bumble is a very intelligent woman who knows what she is talking about,' he said, pressing the ON button so that Kitty's voice drowned out what Mum said next.

'*Hello and welcome to Shortfleet!*' came the warm and friendly tones. '*This CD will tell you a bit about the animals as we go round. After you've finished in each*

enclosure there will be a beeping noise. When you hear that noise, turn the CD off and turn it on again when you reach the next enclosure. At the end of your visit, please feel free to take this CD home, or alternatively you can recycle it by handing it back to one of the keepers on your way out. Remember to observe the safety rules, keep your windows closed and stay inside your vehicle at all times. And, above all, enjoy your visit!'

BEEP!

'So where do we go first?' asked Felix. 'Can we see the monkeys?'

Flo nudged Felix and giggled hysterically.

'Shhh,' he hissed.

Flo bit her lip and forced the giggles back down.

'The monkeys are near the park exit,' said Mum, looking at the map the keeper had given Dad with the CD and tickets.

'So? Can't you drive there first?' Flo asked.

'No,' said Mum firmly, 'You have to follow all the other cars around in a queue – you're not

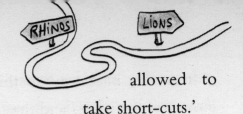

allowed to take short-cuts.'

Flo huffed and slumped back in her seat, but quickly perked up as Dad began following an orange-and-black tiger-striped minibus into the giraffe enclosure.

Every square centimetre of Felix literally tingled with happiness. This was dreamy – a whole day of looking at giraffes, rhinos, lions, tigers, wolves and, of course, monkeys . . . The best was yet to come, he thought with satisfaction, swiftly checking his rucksack to see if the peanuts were easily to hand.

'You have got the bananas Mum gave you, haven't you, Zed?' he asked softly.

'Right here, dude,' Zed said, patting the bag on his lap. 'You hungry?'

'Erm, not yet,' said Felix. 'Oh, look! Wolves!'

Dad had driven through some big metal gates that had notices all over them saying how dangerous the wolves were.

184

'It is very interesting to think that the mothers look after the babies and the fathers go and do the hunting, isn't it?' said Felix, listening to the CD. 'I mean, it's a bit like humans in Real Life, isn't it? Mum looks after me and Merv, and Dad goes out all day to the office.'

'Ahem,' Mum said, turning round and fixing her younger son with a pointed look. 'I happen to go to work too, you know.'

'I know that,' said Felix impatiently. 'But you do look after me too, whereas Dad only goes to work.'

'Hey!' Dad objected. 'You make it sound easy!'

Zed held up his hands. 'Cool it, guys. Life's not a competition. Look at

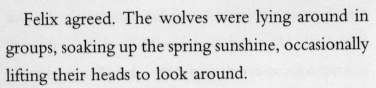

those wolves – they know how to chill out.'

Felix agreed. The wolves were lying around in groups, soaking up the spring sunshine, occasionally lifting their heads to look around.

After an hour of trailing after the stripy tiger bus and listening to the soft, almost sleep-making, tones of Kitty Bumble explaining the individual habits of every animal on the planet, Felix at last spotted a sign that told him they had arrived at the part he had been waiting for.

'MONKEYS!' he yelled.

Flo screeched in delight and Dad quickly turned up the volume on the CD player to cover up the noise. Kitty Bumble's smiley voice warned them that the monkeys were '. . . *quite playful and liable to climb on to your vehicle. Do not be alarmed – as long as you keep your doors and windows shut at all times you will be perfectly safe. If at any time you are anxious and require the assistance of a keeper, simply sound your*

horn and someone will be with you immediately. Please remember to stay inside your vehicle, and be advised that Shortfleet accepts no responsibility for damage to your belongings. Have a great visit in the monkey enclosure!'

Dad let the car slow down a bit. Mum glanced at him questioningly.

'What's the matter?' Felix asked, sensing the tension.

'Erm,' said Dad quietly, 'I'm not sure I want to go in there after all. What if the monkeys do damage the car? I've heard awful stories about people losing their wing mirrors and windscreen wipers.'

Flo gasped and Felix felt a shiver run down his spine.

'Oh, come on, Ian, this car is hardly our pride and joy. We'll have a riot on our hands if we don't go in,' Mum added, glancing over her shoulder at the back seat.

'It will be OK, Mr Stowe,' added Flo with complete certainty. 'I have seen this part of the park on that utterly brilliant programme called *Safari Park Live*, and they absolutely definitely never show monkeys destroying cars.'

'Well, they wouldn't, would they?' Dad grumbled.

But Mum shot him one of her looks, and so he had to drive on, gritting his teeth so hard that Felix noticed the veins in his jaw throbbing in a freaky kind of way. He also noticed his dad press the window lock so that only he could open the windows.

Zed laughed. 'Maybe the monkeys are trying to tell us something, y'know?'

'No, Clive,' said Mum. 'I don't know.'

'Well, like, maybe monkeys have already worked out that cars are bad for the environment and they are trying to tell the guys here that by jumping all over them?'

'Clive,' said Mum, 'shut up.'

'Only if you stop calling me Clive, sis,' Zed said, raising one eyebrow and sitting back in his seat.

Flo took advantage of the boring grown-up-style argument going on to lean in to Felix and loudly whisper, 'I'll give the signal.'

Felix frowned hard at Flo and mouthed, 'NO! I'm giving the signal!'

'What are you two up to *now*?' Mum asked irritably. 'Just sit still. We're going into the enclosure now – look, the gates are opening. And listen to the CD, can't you? That "extremely intelligent" Kitty woman is going to tell us all the fascinating facts she knows about the fascinating monkeys and all their fascinating monkey habits,' she added in a tone of  voice that suggested she didn't really mean what she was saying.

'Can I have a banana?' Felix asked his uncle.

'Yes, me too,' Flo added, staring at Felix in a bit of an Obvious Way. 'I'm utterly starving.'

'Here you are. Not going to feed them to the monkeys, I hope!' Zed said, laughing.

Flo shook her head violently. 'Absolutely not. What a stupid idea,' she said. Felix quickly stuffed a piece of banana into his mouth to prove a point.

Dad drove the car cautiously through the gates which were manned by cheery-looking keepers in T-shirts bearing the red-and-white Shortfleet logo. Flo bounced up and down and waved at the keepers. Felix would normally have joined in, but he was starting to feel distinctly nervous about his plan. Especially now Dad had put the window lock on. Felix stared at the lock and wondered how he was going to be able to unlock it. And how would he be able to tell Flo what to do quickly enough to stop Mum or Dad spoiling things? He fiddled with a bag of peanuts and clutched a banana a bit too hard. *SQUELCH!* It sort of popped and a glob of it squidged out on to his jeans. He felt quite hot and itchy and suddenly wished Dad would put his foot down after all about not going into the monkey reserve. Maybe he should tell Dad that he was worried about the monkeys destroying the car as well? Maybe he should say he felt sick and needed to get out of the car? Maybe he should scream for help—

'They are funny, aren't they? Those two look like they're playing tag!' said Dad, pointing to a cute, soft monkey who was repeatedly tapping his friend on the shoulder and then running

off at top speed before he could be caught.

'Oh man, look at the car in front!' Zed said. 'They're all over the roof! And they're grooming each other! I just love it when they scratch themselves.' He chuckled. 'Look at their long arms. They crack me up. They are so funny!'

'You've gone very quiet, Felix. Don't you like them?' Mum asked, turning round.

Felix shrugged and tried to look Cool and Calm.

'Phew, am I glad our car doesn't have a roof-rack or anything,' Dad said. 'See that caravan up in front – the one with the orange canoes on it? The monkeys are having a ball up there.'

Felix peered through the windscreen to where Dad was pointing. The monkeys certainly were having a ball – dancing in and out of the canoes, ripping bits off them. And nibbling them! What on earth could be tasty about a canoe, Felix wondered idly. Come to that, why would someone want to take canoes into a safari park, anyway? Forget the monkeys, it was people that were odd, Felix decided.

The monkeys very quickly made up their minds that there actually wasn't much to be recommended

192

about the flavour of orange plastic, and they hopped out and started ripping bits of rubber from around the windows of the caravan instead.

'My goodness,' said Mum in horror. 'Are they actually *eating* that?'

But before anyone could agree or disagree: 'Oh look, Felix. Look!' Flo cried, grabbing on to his sleeve and pulling him towards her side of the car. 'There are BABIES! We must get the babies.'

The minute Flo said the word 'babies', lots of things happened at once. Afterwards Felix could not think what had happened first and all the events got jumbled up into his mind in a big panicky tangle. He knew that he had stopped worrying and started to giggle when he saw a crowd of monkeys jabbering and gesturing to each other and running towards his dad's car. And Zed had definitely laughed too and said, 'Man, those apes are going, like, APE!' And he was pretty sure that it was while Dad was jamming on the brakes and the monkeys were cackling and pinging the windscreen wipers at each other and Mum was screaming and flinging her arms around her face, that Flo chose her moment to quietly reach forward to the window controls in the arm rest on Dad's door and press all the buttons at once.

What impressed Felix, and what he was sure he would never forget, was the speed at which the monkeys took over. His plan had not needed so much Careful Forethought after all. He had assumed that the monkeys would be shy of humans and that they would need Coaxing and Tempting to convince them to get into the car. But they hadn't needed anything at all in the way of encouragement. It had not taken the smallest shake of a bag of peanuts or the tiniest wave of a banana skin to entice them – the opening of the car windows had been invitation enough.

Felix had the impression that up until that point events had happened in slow motion with the sound turned off. He was sure he was actually standing outside it all, and watching it like a person on the street watching a telly screen in a shop window.

But the instant the monkeys started pouring into the car, the volume went up full blast and the action sped up to full throttle.

'Quick, Felix, grab one!'

'I can't! They're too fast and – OW! – scratchy!'

'WHO OPENED THE WINDOWS?'

'*Monkeys such as these tend to live in family groups and enjoy grooming—*'

'GET THEM OFF ME!'

'Chill, guys. Remember what Kitty Bumble said—'

'But we have STAYED IN THE VEER-KUL!'

'AAAIIIEEE! THEY'RE PULLING MY HAIR!'

The car was full of monkeys: big ones, small ones, fat ones, baby ones, smelly ones – actually they were all smelly.

'SOUND THE HORN – QUICK!'

It was Mum that said that, Felix was pretty sure. It was difficult to tell, though, as all he could see were monkeys' tails and monkeys' teeth, monkeys' hands and monkeys' bottoms. So many monkeys' bottoms. And the noise. Oh, the noise. It was worse than Felix's worst ever nightmare about being eaten alive by fire-breathing, roaring piranha fish.

'THE HORN, IAN – THE HORN!'

Yup, that was definitely Mum, thought Felix, as he screwed his eyes tight shut and tried in vain to get the car seat to swallow him up and take him away from there.

PAAAARRRRRP!

The horn sounded, Flo screamed an ear-splittingly

horrific scream and the monkeys joined in.

This was what it must be like being a soldier right in the middle of a horrendous battle zone, Felix thought. If not, facing Mum (if he ever got out of there alive) would most certainly be.

The next noise Felix heard was a sound like an ambulance or an air-raid siren. He had seen a film once about evacuees in the Second World War, so he knew what an air-raid siren sounded like. Maybe this *was* a war zone. And who was that screaming?

It took Felix a couple of seconds to realize that it was his own scream he could hear.

His door was wrenched open and hands grabbed at the monkeys skittering around inside the car. Seeing as one of them was connected to Felix's hair, that made him scream quite a lot louder. He found himself wondering if the monkeys had got hold of Flo's hair and hoped very much that they had not. Thank goodness Dad was mostly bald apart from those tufty bits around his ears. If this was how mean monkeys could be, Felix found himself thinking he had quite firmly made up his mind that he did not actually want a monkey as a pet any more. Why did they look so cute if they were really so horrible? Colin was not this bad, even on a Bad Day. In fact, even Merv was nicer than this lot.

'Stay calm!' a voice ordered. 'The more noise you make, the more excitable the monkeys will be.'

'*Stay calm?*' That was Mum, Felix told himself. At least she was still alive. Felix was staring hard at his knees as someone prised a monkey from his head so he couldn't see what was going on around him. 'Stay CALM, did you say? I am being scalped alive by fifty-six million apes and you tell me to STAY CALM!!!'

'Yes, madam,' came the reply.

Gradually the chattering and shrieking and pulling and scratching subsided and Felix was able to raise his head from his knees and look up to see some people dressed in dark green tops and army-type trousers putting monkeys into cages and helping Felix's mum and dad and Zed and Flo out of the car.

The army had come to rescue them!

16

MONKEYS BEHIND BARS

The Stowes and Zed and Flo were ushered into a zebra-striped minibus and the caged monkeys were put into a white van.

'Wh-where are you taking us?' Felix shakily asked.

'We are the keepers who work in the monkey enclosure,' said one of the green-clad people. Oh, so not the army then, Felix thought. He was glad he had not said anything about the army or soldiers or anything. That would have been embarrassing.

'We'll take you to First Aid and then there's someone who needs a word with you. We have to find out exactly what happened so we can make a report,'

another keeper said gruffly. He was a very tall, thickset scary-looking man. A bit like a huge monkey himself, actually, Felix thought. Or a gorilla. In spite of his fear and confusion, a slither of a giggle slipped out.

'I don't know what you are laughing at,' Mum said, her voice encased in a thick layer of ice, 'but if I were you I'd stop right now.'

'Oh, cool it, Marge,' said Zed. 'The boy's stressed. He's been through enough already.'

'Don't you "cool it, Marge" me!' Mum snapped, her eyes glinting dangerously. 'This is all your fault, *Clive*. If you hadn't taken him on all those wildlife-watching expeditions of yours, and if you hadn't encouraged Felix to keep a fully fledged menagerie in his bedroom, and if you hadn't adopted him an orang-utan, then perhaps we would not be on our way to face the music at the head office of Shortfleet Safari Park with a head full of fleas and goodness knows what else!'

Everyone was staring at Mum with their eyes wide open in a terrified expression, and Felix was sure he had stopped breathing. Even Flo was completely speechless for the first time in her life. Her face had gone quite white with fright.

Felix was worried that perhaps Mum was about to hit Uncle Zed. The driver of the minibus called out cheerily over his shoulder: 'Sounds like you've got a regular David Attenborough in the family.'

'David who?' Felix asked, feeling braver at the tone in the man's voice.

'David Attenborough. He's a famous naturalist. You should watch some of his wildlife films. He did a brilliant series about creatures who live in the sea called *The Blue Planet*.'

'Really?' Felix sat up straight, perking up. He leaned towards the driver. 'Can you get it on DVD?'

'Yeah, mate. I think you can get hold of it at—' The man broke off when he caught sight of Mum.

'Do you know,' Mum said slowly and menacingly, 'I don't think at this moment in time that we are very interested in that particular DVD, thank you very much.'

Felix was going to protest, but the sight of Mum with her hair ruffled and her make-up smudged in a clowny fashion and her clothes a bit ripped and that Extremely Dangerous Glint in her eye sort of made him stop and think. He had a sinking feeling that Mum would be keeping a very Tight Rein on his animal-based activities from now on.

The monkeys had apparently gone to First Aid too. Mum mumbled something about them not needing any medical attention, as they had seemed 'very much in tip-top condition'. But the keepers were worried that the monkeys might have injured themselves while they were charging around.

'They could have turned on each other if they had become really panicked,' the gruff gorilla-like keeper told Felix. He led them to a grey Portakabin where they would have their scratches and bruises looked at. 'What you did was extremely stupid,' the keeper went on. 'There are notices all over the park telling you to stay in your vehicle and not to wind down the windows or attempt to feed the animals. Did you not see them? And you should have been listening to instructions on the CD.'

'We did see the notices, and we did listen to the CD,' Mum said, tight-lipped with fury.

Flo was crying quietly at this point, and Zed had his arms round her and kept offering her tissues. Her hair had gone into mega-fluff overdrive and she had peanuts in it and mushed-up banana on her face.

'I wish Silver was here,' she whispered.

'So do I, man. So do I,' Zed said.

The keeper told them to sit on some orange plastic chairs and wait for the First Aid people. Felix's chair had a wobbly leg. He held on to the sides to steady it and felt something sticky under the right-hand edge of the seat. Chewing gum. He prised his fingers free and rubbed them together to get the gum off, but it just made them stickier and stickier.

Two kindly-looking people came and checked them over and gave them plasters and bandages and made Mum and Dad a cup of tea with loads of sugar in it. 'For the shock,' they told them. Felix took a sip and spat it out. Then the keeper came back into the cabin and said, 'There's someone wants a word with you lot. Wait here.'

Felix wiped his sticky hand down his jeans. Mum tapped her foot irritably on the grey lino floor. Flo blew her nose loudly. Zed hummed. Dad coughed.

A fly buzzed right into Felix's face and made for his nose. As he was batting it away and starting to get annoyed with its persistent buzzing and nose-attacking, the door to the Portakabin opened.

The man who entered was more bizarre than any

of the exotic species that Felix had seen at the park that day. He was almost as wide as he was tall, he had long grey hair and an even longer grey beard. He was wearing a floor-length coat that looked as though it had been made out of bits of carpet, huge billowy trousers like a genie in a pantomime and his fingers were covered in massive chunky rings. On

his head was an Olden-Fashioned-Days type of hat, made of black velvety-soft fabric with golden swirls all over it – and in his right hand he held a posh-looking cane with a silvery top in the shape of a fox's head. The man looked like an over-the-top version of one of Zed's mates from down at the canal. Or one of the Wise Men from the nativity play at school. Felix stole a glance at Zed. He certainly looked impressed.

'Well, hello there!' the man boomed, waving a bejewelled hand merrily in the air. 'So who's been the naughty one then? Letting my monkeys into your car? Goodness gracious me, we can't have that, you know!' And he let out a huge wheezy bellow of a laugh.

This man is quite obviously a bit of a loony, thought Felix. He didn't know whether that realization cheered him up or frightened the pants off him. Did the man really find the situation amusing, in which case no one would get into trouble and they could all just have a jolly good laugh about it (well, maybe not ALL, Felix thought, catching sight of Mum's thunderous face). Or was this bizarre-looking man about to blow up at everyone and tell them that they were sentenced to fifty-five years behind bars in a dark and smelly prison millions of miles away?

Felix shuddered. His teacher could be unpredictable like that. Mr Beasley couldn't actually send anyone to be behind bars for fifty-five years (or even one year), of course, but he did have that rather disconcerting habit of laughing like a

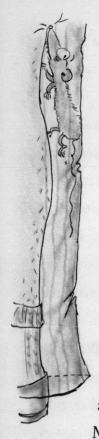

hyena when someone had done something he didn't like, and then exploding with uncontrollable anger two seconds later. Like the time Freya Potts had by mistake let Jeff, the class mouse, out of his cage when it was her turn to clean it out, and the mouse had run right up Mr Beasley's trouser leg in fright. Mr Beasley had howled with laughter to start with, but the minute Freya admitted that it had been her fault he went a deep purple in the face and his nose looked a bit sweaty all of a sudden and then his eyes bulged really quite a lot and he shouted, 'FREYA POTTS! SEE ME AFTER CLASS!'

He had made poor Freya go around on her hands and knees picking up every single pencil shaving, fleck of dust and stray Bit of Grot off the classroom floor. And that is not a nice job when you are in the same class as Humphrey Darling who is responsible for most of the Grot in Freya's class, being as he is the Number One World Champion in Nose Picking and Bogey Flicking.

Felix closed his eyes and took a deep breath and waited for the Mr Beasley-type explosion to occur.

But it didn't. The strange man came over to Felix and slapped him on the shoulder and bellowed his great booming laugh again.

'So this is the younger generation's answer to David Attenborough, is it?' he chortled. 'No need to look so terrified, young man.'

Felix had a sudden exciting thought. Was this man perhaps Father Christmas in disguise? He did sound quite a lot like Father Christmas, and that beard . . . But it was May, so Father Christmas was sleeping, wasn't he? He shook his head and tried to concentrate on what the man was saying.

'Do you know who I am?' he was asking.

Mum and Dad were shuffling their feet and staring at the ground.

He IS Father Christmas! Felix thought, excitement rocketing up from his belly to his face and breaking out in a beaming grin. 'Yes!' he cried. 'You're—'

'Lord Basin!' Zed yelled, jumping up and clapping his hands like a little kid.

'Eh?' Flo said, her face crumpled in confusion.

'What?' said Felix.

'Lord Basin!' Zed cried again. He began pumping Lord Basin's hand in both of his own and burbling: 'Oh man! I thought it was you, but then I thought, No, the dude doesn't come out to meet the public like this, and then when you spoke I thought, like, it must be you, cos you've got such an awesome voice – and that laugh! No one laughs like that. Except maybe Santa! Hahahaha—'

'Clive,' said Mum in a low voice, shooting him one of her dangerous looks.

'No, no, no – it's absolutely tickey-boo!' Lord Basin said, shaking his head and holding up his free hand. 'It's simply glorious of you to say such kind

210

things, my dear chap. And who might you be?'

'Excuse me,' Mum broke in. 'It's very nice of you to be so friendly to us after what's just happened, and I'm sorry to interrupt and everything, but aren't we forgetting something?'

'What's that, my dear lady?' Lord Basin asked, freeing his hand from Zed and taking Mum's and kissing it.

'Oh, erm . . .' Mum blushed and Felix put all his effort into not doing his sick-making thing with his fingers down his throat. The man had kissed his mum! Even Dad didn't do that in public, and he was married to her!

'I – er – I just think that it's important that Felix and Flora here realize the seriousness of their actions and – well, aren't you angry about the monkeys, your, er Lordship?'

'Oh, call me Harry!' boomed Lord Basin, beaming a huge shiny-cheeked grin and winking at her. He bent down slightly to address Felix and Flo.

'So you both let the monkeys in, eh? Fancied one as a pet maybe? Hohoho! What a cheeky pair! You remind me of myself at your age. Er – that is, what exactly *is* your age?' he added, looking suddenly rather puzzled.

Zed chuckled gleefully and Mum rolled her eyes. Dad had found a piece of paper in his pocket which seemed very interesting.

The keeper who had been very quiet until now, broke in at this point: 'With all due respect, Harry, what these children did was extremely dangerous and goes against all the guidelines laid down by Shortfleet. There are notices all over the park—'

'Yes, yes!' said Lord Basin, waving the keeper away impatiently. 'I think they've learned their lesson now, don't you? You can leave us now, Basil.' Basil left looking rather disappointed.

'Basil's right, of course,' he went on, fixing his twinkly eyes on Flo and Felix. 'It *was* a dangerous thing to do. But luckily for you my monkeys are just fine – in fact, if you don't mind me saying so, it's *you* who look the worse for wear after your little encounter. Now, why don't you follow me and you can get cleaned up properly and tell me exactly why you took it into your heads to plan this little adventure in the first place. Then we'll see whether you deserve to be punished – or not!' he added cryptically.

Felix felt himself sliding into Full Panic Mode. The image of a jolly Father Christmas had been replaced in his mind with an evil gobliny jailor – like that slimy guy in *The Lord of the Rings* – who was swinging some heavy rusty iron chains and cackling loudly whilst jeering, 'PUNISHED, MY DEARIES! PUNISHED YOU SHALL BE!'

He glanced at Flo, but she was still

completely silent. Flo could usually talk for England and could probably charm her way out of a tank full of tarantulas, but it seemed that she was no match for a weird old beardy guy in a technicolour dreamcoat and a bucketful of jewellery.

The Stowes, Flo and Uncle Zed trotted obediently after Lord Basin, out of the Portakabin and across the grounds to the huge house that was at the heart of the safari park. It was a very much more subdued party than the one which had set out earlier that day.

17

MONKEY
BUSINESS

Lord Basin's house was as huge as a castle on the outside and as wonderful as a theme park on the inside. It was so wonderful, in fact, that Felix actually realized he was starting to relax as he looked around him. Surely a man who lived in a place such as this could not be a bad type of person?

'Man, this is the most awesome type of awesomeness I have ever dreamed of!' Zed whispered to Felix. 'We are getting a PRIVATE TOUR OF THE DUDE'S HOUSE! Just wait till I tell Silvs.'

'You'll have to excuse me. I like to show off to my guests,' Lord Basin said bashfully, as they reached the front door. 'Dear lady,' he said, turning to Mum and making her blush again, 'would you be so kind as to press this button here?'

Mum did as she was told, pushing
a button set into the stone wall. The
front door immediately slid open,
like those doors in supermarkets, except this door
was not a boring glass one, but a dark solid wooden
one with animals carved all over it.

On the other side of the door it was just as Zed
had said it would be!

There was even the moving carpet Zed had told
them about. Another button in the wall set it in
motion: Flo was allowed to press that one. It made
her smile for the first time since the monkey attack.

'I'd always fancied one of those flying carpets you
hear so much about in charming fairy tales,' Lord
Basin explained, as they stepped on to a length of
Persian rug that began moving like a conveyor belt.
'It's a so much more efficient way of travelling than
simply walking from one end of the house to the
other. For example, I am always leaving my glasses

in the conservatory, which is at the far end of the house, and then realizing I need them once I am in the library, which is at this end. I used to have to walk back and forth, which became exceedingly annoying and such a waste of time, and so I had this moving carpet installed. It's rather wonderful, don't you agree?'

The carpet passed door upon door in a corridor that seemed never-ending, until finally Lord Basin tapped a swirly bit of the carpet's pattern with his cane and they came to a stop outside one of the doors.

'Young man, your turn, I think?' Lord Basin said, pointing to yet another button.

Zed reached out his hand eagerly, but Lord Basin gently restrained him with a bejewelled finger, saying, 'I meant the youngest of the young men,' and nodded to Felix.

Felix grinned and pressed the button. It made the oak door swing back to reveal a richly decorated room with animal-patterned rugs, cushions and furniture and a huge portrait of Lord Basin himself hung over the fireplace.

Felix secretly wished they could have carried on exploring the whole building, but it was clear that Lord Basin wanted them to stop in this room. He gestured to them to sit down on the soft plumped-up cushions. Felix eyed a zebra-striped chair uneasily.

'It's all right – it's not *real* zebra skin!' Lord Basin said, reading Felix's thoughts. 'As if I would have real animal skin in my house – dear me no. My whole life has been dedicated to the *preservation* of endangered species! But I do like a bit of pizzazz – a bit of bling, you know!' he added, winking at Mum.

Mum tittered and it was Dad's turn to roll his eyes.

Felix decided that next birthday he would ask

for a chair just like that.

Lord Basin turned to Felix. 'So who is going to tell me what happened in the monkey enclosure?' he asked, suddenly very serious.

'It was all his idea,' Flo blurted out, pointing at Felix. 'He is *obsessed* with animals. It is all he ever talks about. And you see he got this actually very stupid idea about adopting an elephant and when he realized that it was not going to work because of how big elephants were he decided to adopt an orang-utan and then that didn't work either and so he said to me, "Let's kidnap the monkeys at Shortfleet when we go for my birthday!"'

Felix was pleased that his best friend had finally found her voice again. But he was horrified at the actual words that were coming out of her mouth. How could she DO this to him? If Flo had not persuaded him in the first place that it would be cool to have their very own elephant, none of this would have happened. He was so shocked he could not find a single word in his brain with which to defend himself. He sat there, shaking his head very quickly and trying to remember how to breathe.

Zed was staring at Flo in an equally stunned manner.

Lord Basin did a good job of maintaining a serious expression in the face of his silenced guests and said, 'Ah . . . so it's your birthday, young man? Why didn't you say so? We must have cake . . . lemon or chocolate?'

'Chocolate!' said Flo, beaming.

'Now hang on a minute,' Mum said, standing up in front of Flo and putting her hands on her hips. 'I think you're forgetting a few important details here, Madam.' Things were bad if Mum was calling her that to her face, Felix thought grimly. 'It was you who started Felix on this whole adoption thing and it was YOU, *dear brother –*' she said this as if she didn't really mean it – 'who agreed to do the adopting and who didn't explain it all thoroughly to poor Felix. So I don't actually think any of this is Felix's fault.'

Lord Basin had abandoned all hope of staying serious by now and was clutching his sides and shaking. Then he started roaring with laughter, until tears rolled down his cheeks. 'Come now, dear lady,' he said at last. 'Calm yourself. I am not going to punish anyone for today's little escapade. I think it shows great entrepreneurial spirit and adventure – something we don't see a lot of these days. You should be proud of your son and his little friend here. They will make a great contribution to the preservation of the wildlife on this planet in time, I'm sure.'

Zed nodded and was about to add some words of his own, but Mum shook her head at him in warning.

'And now, let's forget all about it for a moment and get down to some much more important business.' Lord Basin pressed another button in the wall, and a man in a black suit arrived with a trolley full of cakes and drinks.

'Happy birthday, Felix!' Lord Basin cried, lifting the lid of the cake stand with a flourish.

The animal-print cushions were comfy and the hot chocolate was creamy and soothing. Felix had not realized how hungry he was until the cakes arrived. It had been a long time since breakfast.

Soon everyone had forgotten to be cross or nervous or awestruck and they were chatting away with Lord Basin. Felix told him all about his wish to have as many pets as he could fit into his house and his constant battles with Mum.

'And so you see that is why I got very excited when I thought I would be adopting a Wild Endangered Animal for real. Cats and dogs are all very well, but they are not exactly very Different or Exotic and Interesting.'

Mum told him she did not want any more animals unless it was 'over her dead body'.

'The problem is, Lord Basin – er, Harry – that we have a relatively small house and garden and there just isn't the room to accommodate Felix's growing collection of wildlife.'

Then Flo chipped in and told him in detail about their elephant adoption plans right from the beginning.

Finally Zed told him of his trips to Africa with Silver and how he longed to go back. 'Life is a journey after all, man, you know? And Silvs and me, we're not sure we want to let the journey stop just yet.'

Dad sat back and pretended to listen to it all while actually falling fast asleep.

'Well, well, well,' said Lord Basin, leaning into his cushions and resting his huge hands on his even huger belly. 'I can see how passionate you two children are. I know it's hard to believe, Felix, but I was once a young boy just like you; always getting into trouble for bringing unwanted animals home. Of course I was lucky enough to live in this vast place, which meant it was easier to hide the creatures I loved for a while without my dear mum and dad (bless their souls) finding out. But it became more and more difficult to explain away things like huge lumps of poo on the carpet in the dining room (I used to let my St Bernard dog sleep under the grand piano at night).' Flo and Felix shook their heads in amazement. 'And then there were the tortoises – I used to put them to bed for the winter in the oak chests we kept blankets and sheets in. If ever we had guests, someone would go to fetch some spare blankets and more often than not they'd disturb one of my tortoises. That never went down very well. The tortoises weren't too pleased either!'

Felix chuckled. He was transfixed. He had

never met a grown-up like Lord Basin before. Not even Zed would have thought of putting hibernating tortoises into a blanket chest.

'So *that's* why you started the safari park,' Felix said eventually. 'And how did you get the lions and things? Did you actually go to Africa and capture them?'

'Good gracious me, NO!' roared Lord Basin, slapping his thigh, and making Felix jump. 'That would be a terrible thing to do. I did travel in Africa, as you know, and I greatly appreciated seeing the wonderful animals there in their natural habitat. But I also learned of the terrible things that happened to many of them – being hunted for their skins, tusks and so forth. It started me thinking, though, about conservation and what I could do to help protect those poor endangered species. And then something marvellous happened . . .' He paused and leaned forward conspiratorially.

'What?' cried Flo, bouncing impatiently in her seat.

Lord Basin beamed and went on: 'Many years ago, a beautiful film was made about lions in the wild; the lions that were used in that film were bred in captivity. After the filming, there was some debate as to where the lions would go. Some said they should live in London Zoo, for example, and some said they should go and work in a circus. I hated the idea! Poor glorious creatures, shut away in cages! I came back to Shortfleet that night and looked around me and thought, I've enough room here for a few lions of my own . . .

'That's when I came up with the idea of a safari park. Cages are so restricting and harmful to animals, and yet humans have been keeping animals locked away for years. So I thought it might be fun to turn the whole idea upside down and to have humans themselves shut inside a cage and have the animals roaming about freely instead.'

'Humans in *cages*?' Flo scoffed. 'But there aren't any *cages* in your safari park.'

'Are there not?' Lord Basin asked, a merry glint in his eye.

Flo pulled down the corners of her mouth and shrugged her shoulders.

Felix thought about the way they had travelled around the park, and how the wolves had looked at them lazily from their lush green beds of grass, and how the monkeys had invaded the car and attacked them and they had not been able to do anything about it, because they had been trapped . . .

'Hey! I get it – man, that's awesome,' Zed cried, clapping his hands together.

'Yes!' shouted Felix,  suddenly clicking. 'The *cars* are the cages – WE are in the cages. That's it, isn't it?' he said.

Zed was nodding enthusiastically. 'I always said

cars were like artificial constructs that constrain the rhythm of our natural movement, yeah? Well, Harry here is right on it – WE are the captives, man! Shut up in our metal boxes: the lions and that – they get to stare at us in our cages while they get to roam free. Sweet!'

Mum smiled at her brother and shook her head in mock despair.

'So, Felix. What am I going to do with you now?' Lord Basin asked teasingly. 'My keeper who picked you up thinks I should fine you and tell you never to set foot in my safari park ever again . . . but I don't think so. I'm sure you've learned your lesson about tampering with wildlife. Those monkeys are mighty fearsome little rascals once they've got their sights on something, and they played havoc with your dad's car, didn't they? Not to mention poor little Flossie's hair—'

'Erm, it's Flo, actually,' Flo interrupted.

Lord Basin grinned. 'Well, Miss Flo Actually,

228

how about if I tell you what I've been thinking while we've been chatting, and let's see if you agree with me.'

Felix felt his head go into a spin. He gripped the arm of the sofa as hard as he could to stop himself from being sick. He wasn't sure he could handle any more surprises. He suddenly wished he hadn't eaten so many of those cakes.

'How would you like to come back to Shortfleet some time soon and be keeper for the day and learn how to look after my animals properly? Once you've seen how much hard work goes into caring for wild animals, you'll be in a better position to think about  whether that is what you really want to do when you grow up.'

Felix's jaw dropped to the ground and Flo squealed.

'I take it you like the idea?' Lord Basin said, his eyes twinkling. 'There's one more thing. I would like to give you a birthday present, Felix. That is, if it's all right with you, dear lady?' he asked Mum.

She shrugged awkwardly and Felix felt his insides jump around in excitement.

'Felix, I am touched by your story about Reggie,' Lord Basin continued. 'I hate to think of your disappointment when you learned you wouldn't be taking him home to live with you. I would like to do something to remedy that. Now, obviously I can't give you one of my monkeys to take home. You've seen what little devils they can be, and they need to be looked after by properly trained keepers . . . however, I very much like the idea of the adoption scheme, and so I've been thinking while we've been chatting – how about you adopt one of my animals? You can choose any animal you like: any size, any colour. The animal will stay here, of course, but you can come and visit it and help at

230

cleaning-out and feeding times whenever you like.'

Felix gulped and squeezed his eyes tight shut and then opened them again. He pinched himself hard on the arm for good measure. 'Ow! ... Er, wow!' he cried. 'I'm not dreaming then? Oh . . . oh, my . . .' Before he could stop to think, he leaped up from the cushions and ran round and round the room thumping the air and yelling, 'This is the best birthday ever!'

'Like, crazy, man!' said Zed, clapping his hands and laughing.

Lord Basin was laughing his booming laugh too, his belly shaking as he watched Felix do another victory lap of the room.

Mum coughed nervously and said, 'Well, that's awfully kind of you, Lord Ba—'

'Harry!' Lord Basin reminded her.

Mum nodded shyly. 'Erm, that's awfully kind of you, Harry, but I really think—'

'Listen, my dear,' Lord Basin interrupted, gently

231

placing a giant hand on Mum's arm, 'I love to encourage youngsters to get involved with conservation, and your son has a real passion, surely you can see that? It would be an honour to have him here at Shortfleet on a regular basis. Now,' he said, turning to Flo, 'what about you, Miss Flo Actually? Do you think you would like to come along and help out too?'

A smile spread slowly over Flo's banana-clad features and she said, 'I think I could manage that.'

'Good, that's settled then,' said Lord Basin. 'Just so long as you both remember one very important thing.'

'What's that?' Felix asked.

'Next time you visit – no monkey business!'

A MESSAGE FROM THE AUTHOR

My son ran out of school one afternoon with the exciting announcement that he and his friends were going to open their own zoo!

'We've decided we'll have zebras, giraffes and elephants in the garden,' he told me breathlessly. 'And the seals can go in our pond. But don't worry, Mum,' he said, patting me on the arm reassuringly, 'I've said the snakes will have to go to Jamie's, as I know you don't much like reptiles.'

I chuckled to myself, thinking how wonderful it was that my son and his friends had such active imaginations. I even went so far as to encourage him in his dream by asking him what other animals he thought would be good additions to his zoo.

However, it very quickly became clear that, as far as the boys were concerned, this was not a make-believe game at all. Far from it: this imaginary zoo was to become *reality*.

After a couple of weeks of feverish planning and debate, in which my son and his friends spent every waking moment writing lists of desirable zoo animals, researching their habits and feeding requirements on the Internet, and drawing up designs to show where each and every 'enclosure' would need to be built, I tentatively asked where the boys were going to get all these creatures from exactly.

The answer was delivered with a look that quite plainly said: *Are you completely bonkers, Mum?*

'We're going to write to Longleat Safari Park and ask them to give us some, of course,' my son told me. 'They've got loads of animals there. They won't mind giving us a few.'

And so the idea for *Monkey Business* was there, right under my nose! Of course, I had to make up a few things to make it into the story that it is now as, unlike Felix and Flo, my son and his friends thankfully did not go so far as to plan a full-scale kidnapping (or 'monkey-napping') operation!

I did use the Longleat idea, though, for my fictional safari park, Shortfleet. Longleat is a very famous safari park and stately home not far from where I live. It is owned by Lord Bath who, just like Lord Basin in my story, decided to give a home to lions that had been used in the making of a film. It was in doing this that Lord Bath created the first location outside Africa to open a drive-through safari park. You can find out more about Longleat and all the animals there at www.longleat.co.uk.

However, UNLIKE Lord Basin, Lord Bath would definitely *not* be as easily forgiving if you tried to take any of the animals out of the park, so if you are ever lucky enough to go to Longleat, *please* obey all the rules of the safari park and do not try any monkey business!

My son never did get his own zoo, although he hasn't quite given up hope. At the last count we had one dog, two cats, two chickens, and a pond full of water boatmen, shrimps, frogspawn and pond skaters. And there has been talk recently of acquiring a hamster or a guinea pig or two . . .

I hope you enjoyed this story. If you would like to find out more about me and my books, please visit www.annawilson.co.uk. Or you can write to me:

> Anna Wilson
> c/o Macmillan Children's Books,
> 20 New Wharf Road,
> London
> N1 9RR

Love
Anna
xxx

PS I'd love to see your pet photos too! But don't forget to enclose a stamped addressed envelope if you want me to return them to you.

A MESSAGE FROM THE ILLUSTRATOR

When I was told that Anna Wilson's next book would be called *Monkey Business*, I got lots of paper out and practised drawing little monkeys, making them as cute and cuddly as I could. You see, the other books

I've illustrated for Anna were all about puppies and kittens, so naturally my brain was set on fluff and big soppy eyes. But it didn't turn out that way, did it? This book is alive with creepy-crawlies and warty toads and sick hamsters, and cows doing what cows do. Elephants fly, wolves tell jokes, and fish hurtle down the toilet. And the monkeys? I only managed to get ONE cute one in. And then, see what it did!

Moira Munro

Anna Wilson

I, Summer Holly Love, have wished a million thousand times for a puppy of my own, for ever and ever, AMEN.

So I was over the top of the moon with happiness when I finally obtained Parental Consent to get Honey – the most absolutely softest and velvetest puppy in the whole world. Although being a pet owner is not the most easiest trick in the book. Honey and I have had some Extremely Entertaining adventures together. (Like the time we had to deal with my weird sister April's cringesome love crush on Honey's vet . . .)

The first hilarious, slightly barking mad book about Summer and Honey

Anna Wilson

Pup Idol

Our second truly amazing book, in which Honey goes
through her Awkward Adolescence – in other words,
develops a taste for shoes (mainly flip-flops), and for
raiding our fridge and terrorizing dinner guests. Mum
is not particularly delighted so Steps Have To Be Taken
and eventually, with a bit of dutiful training, Honey
develops true Star Quality and we all become Famous
Celebrities in Our Own Right at the school talent show.

Anna Wilson

Puppy Power

I never thought I would say this, but life with Honey, my Number One Pooch, had been getting a little bit yawnsome of late. She was still 110 per cent gorgeous, of course, but now that she was TREMENDOUSLY well trained by me, there wasn't exactly much happening in my life on a day-to-day basis.

That is, until Nick Harris, Mr Fantabulous Vet of the Year, came up with the idea of Honey having PUPPIES . . .

**The third brilliant book about
Summer and Honey**

Coming soon

Anna Wilson

Puppy Party

You are Most Cordially Invited –
in other words, PLEASE COME to a

PUPPY PARTY!

On: Friday 13 April

At: Summer and Honey's House

For: Fun, Frolics and Fantastic Snackeroos of a
pooch-type nature!

Bring your owner
(and your lead and pooper-scooper to avoid Mishaps)

And DON'T TELL MUM OR APRIL –
it's a surprise . . .

RSVP in SECRET to Summer ASAP!

**Hold on to your party hats! It's another barking
mad adventure for Summer and Honey!**

Website Discount Offer

Get 3 for 2 on Anna Wilson books at
www.panmacmillan.com

£1 postage and packaging costs to UK addresses, £2 for overseas

To buy the books with this special discount:

1. visit our website, www.panmacmillan.com
2. search by author or book title
3. add to your shopping basket

Closing date is 31 July 2011.

Full terms and conditions can be found at www.panmacmillan.com

Registration is required to purchase books from the website.

The offer is subject to availability of stock and applies to paperback editions only.